TREASURE HUNTERS

THE ULTIMATE QUEST

NO. 1 BESTSELLING AUTHOR
JAMES PATTERSON
and CHRIS GRABENSTEIN

Illustrated by JULIANA NEUFELD

002

Young Arrow
20 Vauxhall Bridge Road
London SW1V 2SA

Young Arrow is part of the Penguin Random House group of companies
whose addresses can be found at global.penguinrandomhouse.com.

First published in the UK by Young Arrow in 2022

www.penguin.co.uk

A CIP catalogue record for this book is available from the British Library

ISBN: 978–1–529–12003–5

Printed and bound in Great Britain by Clays Ltd, Elcograf S.p.A.

The authorised representative in the EEA is Penguin Random House Ireland,
Morrison Chambers, 32 Nassau Street, Dublin D02 YH68

Penguin Random House is committed to a sustainable future
for our business, our readers and our planet. This book is made
from Forest Stewardship Council® certified paper.

TREASURE HUNTERS

THE ULTIMATE QUEST

James Patterson is the internationally bestselling author of the highly praised Middle School, Ali Cross, Jacky Ha-Ha, Treasure Hunters, Dog Diaries and Max Einstein series. James Patterson's books have sold more than 400 million copies worldwide, making him one of the biggest-selling authors of all time. He lives in Florida.

Chris Grabenstein is a *New York Times* bestselling author who has collaborated with James Patterson on the I Funny, Jacky Ha-Ha, Treasure Hunters, House of Robots and Max Einstein series, as well as *Word of Mouse, Katt vs. Dogg, Katt Loves Dogg, Pottymouth and Stoopid, Laugh Out Loud*, and *Daniel X: Armageddon*. He lives in New York City.

Juliana Neufeld is an award-winning illustrator who has worked with James Patterson on the Treasure Hunters and House of Robots series. Her drawings can be found in books, on album covers, and in nooks and [illegible] lives in Toro[illegible]

A list of titles by James Patterson appears at the back of this book

To Alexander ("Andy"),
Nicholas, and Maxwell Balboni
Logan and Bailey Bigelow
Olivia and Aidan Klauk

GREENLAND

BET YOU DIDN'T KNOW A SECRET BEEHIVE WAS BUILT INTO THE CHAPEL! NEAT, HUH?

ROSSLYN CHAPEL SCOTLAND

ATLANTIC OCEAN

CHÂTEAU DE GISORS FRANCE

WORK ON THE CASTLE STARTED IN 1095!

NORTH AMERICA

CALIFORNIA

THE HOTTEST PLACE IN THE USA IS DEATH VALLEY. IT'S REACHED 130°F (THAT'S 54.4°C)!

CENTRAL AMERICA

AFRICA

SOUTH AMERICA

SÃO PAOLO, BRAZIL IS HOME TO MORE PEOPLE THAN ANY OTHER CITY IN SOUTH AMERICA!

ARCTIC OCEAN

THE WORLD ACCORDING TO THE KIDDS

ST. PETERSBURG, RUSSIA
ST. PETERSBURG HAS ALMOST AS MANY BRIDGES AS VENICE, ITALY! THAT'S **ALOT** OF BRIDGES.

RUSSIA

EUROPE

ASIA

MEDITERRANEAN SEA

ISRAEL

ALEXANDRIA, EGYPT
FOUNDED IN **331 BCE!** THAT'S A LONG TIME AGO!

THE DEAD SEA, ON THE BORDER BETWEEN ISRAEL AND JORDAN, IS THE LOWEST POINT ON THE EARTH'S SURFACE! IT MEASURES ABOUT 1,400 FT / 430 M BELOW SEA LEVEL!

THE NILE

AFRICA IS HOME TO THE LONGEST RIVER, THE NILE, WHICH IS 6,852 KM / 4,258 MI. YOU MIGHT REMEMBER IT FROM THE KIDD FAMILY'S TRIP DOWN THE NILE!

PACIFIC OCEAN

INDIAN OCEAN

AUSTRALIA

THE GREAT BARRIER REEF IS THE BIGGEST CORAL REEF IN THE WORLD! IT'S OFF THE COAST OF AUSTRALIA AND HAS OVER 3,000 REEFS AND 900 ISLANDS!

NEW ZEALAND

ANTARCTICA

QUICK NOTE FROM BICK KIDD

Hi! It's me again—Bick Kidd. Just wanted to remind you that I'll be the one telling this story (and it's pretty darn exciting, if I do say so myself, which I just did). My twin sister, Beck—she's the one with the ink-speckled hands—will be doing the drawings.

Okay. Fine. Beck says if I'm going to mention the ink all over her hands I have to mention the orange goop smeared on the tips of my fingers. What can I say? I love a good bag of cheese puffs.

PART ONE

LOST AT SEA

CHAPTER 1

The second time we lost our parents was even worse than the first.

Because we also lost our boat. (Guess that's bound to happen sooner or later when you name your ship *The Lost.*)

Tommy, Beck, and I were flippering around on a dive, exploring the underwater ruins of the sunken city of Thonis-Heracleion. It's a real version of the mythical Atlantis. Thonis-Heracleion was once a sprawling port city that used to be ancient Egypt's gateway to the Mediterranean Sea. Now it's buried under that same sea.

We were approximately 6.5 kilometers (about four miles) off the coast of Egypt, northeast of Alexandria. Our big sister, Storm, was topside in our dive boat. Storm, who has a photographic memory, hates scuba diving. Probably because one of the photographs in her memory is a snapshot of the one time she *did* join us on an underwater treasure hunt. It includes a shark trying to bite her in the butt.

Mom and Dad were on board our ship, *The Lost*, feeding us the data we needed for this dive.

"It's a test run," Dad had explained. "For our next big treasure quest."

"If it works here," said Mom, "it'll guide us to the ultimate treasure. The treasure of all treasures! And it's been missing for more than seven hundred years!"

Mom and Dad are big on building suspense like that. Keeps everybody psyched and highly motivated.

We'd just wound up on a quick expedition in Antarctica. No, we weren't looking for penguin pirate plunder. We were searching for meteorites—chunks of space rocks buried beneath the ice. We'd found several, and our Great Uncle Richie "Poppie" Luccio, who'd been with us on our last couple of treasure hunts (and really is pretty great), had decided to stay at the South Pole with a team of British researchers to look for more space rocks, especially iron meteorites that might come from the interiors of distant planets or the cores of asteroids. Uncle Richie loved the science. He also loved the fact that the British team's members liked to play cards at night. He would be off the grid for weeks.

Meanwhile, Tommy, Beck, and I were testing out some new treasure-hunting gear Mom and Dad had invented: augmented reality dive masks.

It was kind of like that old Pokémon Go game, only way more sophisticated and advanced.

The AR dive masks used tons of data and charts created from high-tech surveying, sonar readings, and archaeological research to overlay an image of what an ancient place used to look like over what was there now. In our case, we could see the outline of an ancient Egyptian

BECK'S MASK VIEW

temple superimposed over what was there now: murky darkness and swirling sand.

Up on the surface, Storm was running the submersible Wi-Fi system that streamed all the data needed to create the augmented reality images projected on the interior glass of our dive masks. That data (and the same kind of information for a "treasure hunt to be announced later," as Mom and Dad put it) was actually stored on a single super laptop computer on board *The Lost*. It had a bajillion-petabyte hard drive. Okay, I made that number up. Let's just say the thing's storage capacity is ginormous.

The AR dive masks are how we had just located a priceless marble statue of Cleopatra, who looked like she'd been holding her breath underwater for more than two thousand years.

Suddenly, all the augmented reality visuals inside our masks disappeared. The glass went blank.

Until we saw a fresh video image: Storm waving her hand over her head.

She wasn't waving "Howdy." She was giving us a dive distress signal.

The one for "trouble on the surface"!

CHAPTER 2

The three of us kicked our way topside as quickly as we could.

The first thing I saw was Storm perched in the bow of the dive boat. She looked horrified. She was also pointing at the horizon.

The second thing I saw was the thing that had horrified Storm: *The Lost*. On the horizon. ON FIRE!

Great big black billowy clouds were boiling up off the stern. The dark and lumpy cloud clumps were chased skyward by orange flames lashing up from the diesel-fueled engines down below.

"Are Mom and Dad okay?" shouted Beck, who had her mask tilted back on her head.

"I don't know!" said Storm. "Their communications cut out the same instant the data stream did."

Tommy was already clambering up into the inflatable rubber raft we used for our dive boat.

"The fire suppression system down in the engine room should've kicked in!" he shouted.

"Well, obviously, it didn't!" said Beck, hauling herself up into the boat with a sideways flop. "Come on, Bick! We need to go put out that fire!"

I grabbed hold of the slick sides of the sixteen-foot dinghy and pulled myself on board.

"I suspect electrical issues," said Storm.

"Impossible," said Tommy, yanking on the outboard motor's starter cord. "Dad and I thoroughly inspected every single wire, switch, electrical outlet, and circuit breaker last week!"

Beck and I exchanged a glance. We wondered if Tommy left his hair dryer running this morning. It's how he keeps his swooping mane so swingy and fluffy.

As we raced (okay, puttered—the dive boat isn't all that fast) across the choppy water and pulled closer to *The Lost*, we could feel the heat radiating off the fireball at the rear of the ship. We could also smell the acrid odor of burning oil and melting rubber.

Then came the explosion.

A tremendous fireball burst through the roof of the wheelhouse.

"That sounded like a bomb!" said Storm.

"You guys?" I said. "This might not be an accident. This might be an attack!"

Storm flashed a Morse code message with her very shiny signal mirror. "Their electronic devices and cell phones don't seem to be working. I'll let them know the old-fashioned way that help is coming."

"Smart thinking, Storm!" said Tommy, twisting the engine throttle as far as he could without snapping it off. The engine whined.

Beck and I were up in the bow. We hoped that Mom and Dad would signal back. Our eyes swept the deck.

We saw nothing.

"Prepare to board, you guys!" said Tommy as he swung the skiff sideways. "Storm? Stay with the raft. Bick and Beck? You're with me."

Storm made her way to the back of the dive boat. Tommy bounded across the bench seats like a long jumper building up speed for his blastoff. He leapt past Beck and me, flew up, grabbed hold of a railing, and hauled himself up onto the deck of *The Lost*. He quickly found a rope and tossed us a line.

Beck and I clambered up to our ship.

When we grabbed the side railings, they were sizzling hot.

We had to find Mom and Dad. Fast.

We were running out of time.

So was *The Lost*.

CHAPTER 3

We used our arms to block the broiling heat rolling in waves off the fiery stern.

Whatever water droplets that had attached themselves to our dive suits and flippers evaporated in an instant. I just hoped our neoprene wet suits wouldn't melt and turn us into shrink-wrapped plastic action figures with only one pose.

"The ship is taking on water!" said Tommy, coming back from a quick inspection of the stern.

"Good!" I said. "The water will put out the fire."

"It will also sink the ship!" said Beck.

"Well, at least it won't be burning any longer."

"Water's no good on an oil fire, Bick," said Tommy. "It'll just spread out on the sea and keep burning until the fuel is all gone."

"The Room!" I shouted. I would've snapped my fingers, too, but that's super hard to do when you're wearing rubber gloves.

"Bick's right!" said Beck. "It's the safest place on the ship!"

Tommy nodded. "Way to think, guys. If Mom and Dad are still on board, that's where they'll be. In The Room!"

The three of us dashed up toward the bow of the boat.

"We'll go in through my cabin!" said Tommy, pulling up on the deck hatch that doubled as his ceiling's skylight.

No smoke came pouring out of the cabin below.

That was a good thing. It meant that, at least for now, the fire was contained to the stern and hadn't plowed its way forward through the galley and all the boat's bulkheads.

We dropped down into Tommy's room.

(I looked. He *had* turned off his blow dryer. His miniature espresso machine, too.)

We split up for a few seconds, each of us poking our heads into the other cabins. Tommy's room. Storm's. Mom and Dad's.

There was nothing. Except the first wisps of curling smoke seeping in under the aft door to the galley.

There was a tremendous groaning, creaking sound as the whole ship began to tilt backward. We heard crashing and clattering and clinking. Whatever wasn't nailed or battened down slid around and rolled off shelves, bookcases, and countertops.

"*The Lost* is going down!" I shouted.

"Well, I'm not the captain," said Beck. "So, no way am I going down with the ship."

"None of us are," said Tommy, who can be incredibly heroic while I'm usually incredibly terrified. When the going gets tough, he has that whole Keep Calm and Carry On thing going on. "But first, we need to inspect...The Room!"

Whenever any of us said "The Room," it was like we had to hold a beat for the DUN-DUN-DUN music. The Room was a supersecret place that was, in the olden days, off limits to *all of us*. It also has a solid steel door with a serious dead bolt—the same kind they use on bank vaults. At Fort Knox.

The Room was where Mom and Dad kept the

most secret stuff on the boat. Treasure maps. Retrieval plans. Notes on dealers and middlemen for museums. Lists of Treasures to Be Hunted. But, when they both went missing after a tropical storm, The Room became ours.

So did The Key to The Room. (Everything about the place needed capital letters.) We made several copies.

Fortunately, I wore mine on a chain around my neck. (It looks cooler than it sounds. Okay. Beck says it looks dorky. Fine. You don't have to draw me dramatically fishing around in my dive suit to retrieve it. Although it'd be awesome if you did.)

The Room was the safest place on the ship because the walls were fireproof. They had to be. There was a lot of important stuff on display and in the file cabinets.

Which, we discovered when I unlocked the door, had been trashed.

Somebody had yanked open all the drawers and tossed papers and folders all over the floor.

"Mom and Dad didn't do this," said Beck. "Somebody else is on this ship."

"Or they were," I added.

There was another moaning creak, and the boat lurched backward again—enough to knock Beck and me off our feet. We fell face-first on the slanted floor.

"We're running out of time," said Tommy. "Mom and Dad are gone."

"How can you be sure?" I asked.

Tommy jutted out his lantern jaw and struck a very heroic pause. "I just am, little brother. I just am."

CHAPTER 4

"What about all the cubbyholes and hiding places back up on deck?" said Beck.

The Lost had all sorts of cool secret compartments where we stowed stuff we didn't want any bad guys knowing about—including some pretty awesome weaponry.

Tommy shook his head. "You don't hide in a secret compartment with walls made out of wood during a blazing inferno, guys. We have to face facts: Mom and Dad are gone and our ship is sinking. We need to grab what we can and abandon ship."

I looked around The Room. There were so many antiques and precious artifacts worthy of being rescued. Sure, some of them were sliding out of their display cases and shattering, but still...

"There's so much to save, Tommy!" shouted Beck. "So many memories."

"I know!" Tommy shouted back.

We all had to shout. The fire was getting closer and louder. The listing *Lost* was creaking and straining and pulling itself apart.

"But, you guys?" Tommy continued. "Sometimes you just have to decide what's really important and go for it!"

Tommy grabbed Dad's laptop as it slid along the top of a tilting desk.

That was a smart move.

The innocent-looking computer was the brains of the whole augmented-reality-treasure-hunting system. Maybe it could, somehow, help us find the most important treasure of all: Mom and Dad.

Beck went for a necklace with a pendant. It was Mom's favorite and the one piece of jewelry Beck had always admired more than any other, including all the diamonds and emeralds and rubies we'd found inside treasure chests.

I grabbed Dad's fake Grecian urn. It was a cheap copper replica of the priceless one that had helped us the last time we lost our parents. Even though it was a chintzy rip-off of the real deal, it reminded me of this corny joke Dad liked to tell (over and over and over): *What's a Grecian urn? About thirty dollars a week.*

"You're rescuing a piece of cheap pottery?" said Beck.

"It's important to me!"

"Well, this necklace is important to me!"

“I didn’t say anything about the necklace, Beck.”

“No, but you were thinking it, Bick!”

“Was not.”

“Were, too!”

“Wasn’t!”

“Were!”

“You guys?” shouted Tommy. “This is no time for a Twin Tirade. It’s time to abandon ship!”

Tommy was right. The boat we’d used to hunt shipwrecks was about to become a wrecked ship itself!

CHAPTER 5

The three of us grabbed whatever handholds we could find on deck and climbed our way up what had become a steep slope as the ship simultaneously angled skyward and slid deeper into the sea.

If you've ever seen the movie *Titanic*, it was sort of like that. But without the music.

The back half of *The Lost* was already underwater and, as Tommy predicted, our fuel spill was still raging, churning out thick plumes of oily black smoke.

We all had to jump overboard to rejoin Storm in the motor-powered rubber raft below.

"We need to get out of here!" Storm advised us after we'd hit the inflatable deck and bounced around like we were at somebody's floating bouncy house birthday party. We only had a minute or two to think about all *The Lost* meant to each of us. It had been our home. Our school. Our playground. We had sailed around the globe with her. We had grown up with her.

It was like we were all losing our oldest and dearest friend.

Just when I was about to start snuffling back the tears, Storm pointed to the sky. And the helicopter hovering overhead.

"We have uninvited visitors!"

"Yikes!" said Beck, freaking out (just a little) and jostling the necklace she'd rescued from The Room (which, by the way, she was already wearing. Don't ask me when she found time to put on jewelry during all that dramatic escaping, but, somehow, she did).

The pendant on the necklace started blinking. A small, strobing red dot of light throbbed inside the faceted jewel.

“I must’ve accidentally bopped some kind of button!” said Beck.

The thumping helicopter dropped down lower and swooped in closer.

“It’s a homing beacon!” shouted Tommy, throttling the outboard engine with a wicked twist of his wrist.

We blasted off, bouncing over the wake *The Lost* was churning up as it slid deeper and deeper into the Mediterranean. “Whoever’s on that chopper is going to use that pendant to target us. Throw it away, Beck! Toss it overboard.”

“No!” shouted Storm. “That’s Mom’s favorite necklace.”

“I know,” said Beck. “That’s why I wanted to save it.”

“Good move.” Storm turned to face Tommy. “No way would Mom put a targeting device on her necklace. But it could be a distress signal.”

“Good,” I said. “Because we’re definitely in distress!”

“Okay, okay,” said Tommy. “Sorry I said ‘toss it,’ Beck. Maybe it’s one of those ‘I’ve fallen and

I can't get up' type devices they advertise on TV. Maybe it'll call for help."

"Let's hope so," said Beck. "Because we could definitely use some. Right now!"

The helicopter dipped into a dive like it wanted to land in our raft.

Tommy goosed the outboard motor and the raft shot off like a surfboard cresting a curl.

"The shore is four miles away," said Storm. "Head south and west, Tommy."

"No can do," said Tommy. "Need to initiate some evasive maneuvers first."

He was right. The helicopter was still chasing after us. Tommy would try to shake them off our tail with some fancy boatmanship.

I looked back to where *The Lost* used to be. There was nothing left but a greasy, flaming stain on the surface of the water. *The Lost* was, officially, lost. We probably would've all bowed our heads and had a moment of silence for our beloved ship except the noisy helicopter made even momentary silence impossible.

Then someone started yelling out of the

helicopter's side with a bullhorn.

"Children?" came the amplified voice from overhead. "Kidd family members?"

I shielded my eyes and looked up. A woman in a flight suit was perched in the chopper's open cargo door.

"I think she's talking to us," I said.

"Well, duh," said Beck. "There's nobody else down here. Plus, we're the Kidds. Remember?"

Beck was right. And not just about us being the Kidds. We were in the middle of nowhere. There was nothing around us but choppy salt water. No other boats. No rescue helicopters. No cavalry riding speedboats and wave runners to our rescue.

Just the lady overhead with the bullhorn.

"I'm gonna ease up on the throttle," said Tommy. "Hear what she has to say."

And, of course, once Tommy realized it was a woman on the bullhorn, he smiled and struck a pose that showed off most of his muscles. He has a thing for the ladies. It's why Mom and Dad call him Tailspin Tommy. He meets a girl, even one

hanging out of a helicopter with a bullhorn, and he tumbles hopelessly into love.

"How ya doin' up there?" Tommy called out. His teeth, which he whitens on a regular basis, twinkled in the sun.

"Come with us, children!" said the lady. "We'll take you to your parents."

"You know where they are?" shouted Tommy.

"Yes. We rescued them off your boat when it caught fire."

"Cool," said Tommy.

Storm sighed. Very loudly.

"I hate to break your heart, Tommy," she whispered through gritted teeth, "but she's lying. Get us out of here. Now!"

CHAPTER 6

"Excuse me, ma'am," Tommy said with a wink to the lady hanging out of the chopper. "Need to have a family meeting."

"Be quick about it!" the lady blared back through her bullhorn.

"Oh, we will," muttered Storm.

Then the four of us draped our arms over one another's shoulders and, basically, held a football huddle on our raft.

"Tommy?"

"Yes, Storm?"

"Might I remind you that I was topside with the dive boat when the fire erupted on *The Lost*."

"Sure. Thanks for the reminder. 'Preciate it."

"What's your point, Storm?" asked Beck.

"That while you three were underwater visiting Cleopatra in her waterlogged temple, I was the only one in a position to hear an approaching rescue helicopter."

"And did you?" asked Tommy, innocently.

"Uh, no, Thomas. That's how I know your new girlfriend up there is lying."

"She's not really my—"

"The only sounds I heard were the crackle and roar of our boat going up in flames. I suspect that, far from being our saviors, the people in that chopper are connected to whoever kidnapped Mom and Dad and sank our ship!"

Tommy nodded. "Riiiiiight. Excellent deduction, sis."

"Thanks."

We broke our huddle. Tommy returned to the stern and the outboard motor. He rested his right hand on the throttle.

"No, thank you!" he shouted up to the helicopter. "We're good."

"What?" the woman squeaked through her squawk horn.

I cupped my hands around my mouth and shouted, "Sorry. Our parents told us to never accept helicopter rides from strangers."

"Buh-bye!" added Beck, with a snarky wave.

"Kick it, Tommy," said Storm, as we all sat down and grabbed the plastic handles lining the sides of our raft.

Tommy goosed the engine and, once again, we sliced through the sea like a balloon somebody blew up and then let go. We were on a corkscrewing, serpentine trajectory. Tommy was cutting doughnuts in the water, shooting up spray to rival a jet ski.

"Helicopters can only stay aloft for two or two-and-a-half hours," said Storm. "Their gas tanks can only hold so much fuel. Their maximum range is approximately two hundred and fifty miles."

"Chya," said Tommy, who, as you might recall, is working on his pilot's license (mostly by making the rest of us airsick with his unintentional loop-the-loops, barrel rolls, and nosedives).

"We just need to keep running them around in circles until they run out of gas!" said Beck.

Um, couldn't the same thing happen to us? I wanted to ask. But I didn't. This was no time for logic.

Tommy kept executing ridiculously clever evasive maneuvers. The helicopter did its best to keep up with his every move.

While my stomach gurgled and lurched from side to side, I wondered what we were going to do. Mom and Dad were gone. Most likely kidnapped

by some nefarious evildoers or jealous competitors. (We'd met a lot of both on our adventures.) Our other part-time adult supervision provider, Uncle Richie, was unreachable down in Antarctica.

We Kidd kids were on our own. Again.

We'd done okay the last time we lost our parents. Of course, back then, we had a boat. Now all we had was a rubber raft and the dive suits we were wearing. We also had Dad's laptop, Mom's blinking pendant, and, of course, the imitation Grecian urn (retail price, $15.99 on Etsy).

I was starting to wish I had grabbed a can of Pringles from the galley instead. Maybe a bottle of water.

We had no food. No fresh, unsalted water.

I looked up at the helicopter, which, mercifully, had just blocked the blazing sun. The lady was leaning out of the side door again, and this time she had a camera with a long lens and was snapping photos. Satisfied that she had whatever shot she wanted, she stowed the photography gear and pulled up her bullhorn again.

"Very well," she blared, "if you four ungrateful

brats don't want to be rescued we'll just let you die. We don't really need you alive. We just need to convince your parents that we saved you so they'll do what we need done. We'll show them the 'proof of life' picture I just captured!"

"Excellent," said Storm.

"Um, they just said they're going to leave us out here to die," said Beck. "How is that excellent?"

"Because they also just confirmed that Mom and Dad are still alive!"

"Prepare your missile defenses!" the lady advised us.

Tommy cupped his hands around his mouth and shouted up at her. "Um, we really don't have any of those..."

"Oh, too bad. Because I have this!"

She tossed away her bullhorn and swung up a shoulder-fired rocket launcher.

Which she aimed directly at us!

CHAPTER 7

"We only have one missile left, Dame Elizabeth!" I heard someone else shout inside the helicopter.

Yeah. They were that close. Maybe ten yards behind and only a dozen yards above us.

"One is all I need!" yelled the lady with the rocket launcher resting on her shoulder.

"Stand by, Tommy," said Storm, reaching into one of her many pockets for...something.

"Stand by for what?" asked Tommy, who was still making our rubber raft cut all kinds of crazy circles in the sea.

"Incoming," said Storm. She had her eyes narrowed and locked in on Dame Elizabeth, the gunner up in the chopper. "Who knows where she'll fire that rocket." Storm squinted even harder.

"At us!" I said, because you didn't have to be a rocket scientist to plot the missile's upcoming trajectory.

The lady put her finger on the rocket launcher's trigger.

Storm whipped out her shiny silver signal mirror.

She flashed a retina-searing reflection up at Dame Elizabeth and scored a direct hit, frying her eyeballs with blinding light. The lady flinched. Swung to the left. Fired.

The rocket went swirling sideways into the sea, where it exploded harmlessly.

Well, unless you were one of the fish swimming near the impact zone. Then you probably didn't think the whole rocket-hitting-the-Mediterranean-Sea thing was so harmless.

Dame Elizabeth shook her fist at us as the helicopter banked hard to the right and motored away.

"Woo-hoo!" shouted Beck. "Way to go, Storm! You, too, Tommy! You ran them around in circles until they almost ran out of gas!"

I raised my hand to slap Tommy a high five.

He left me hanging.

Probably because the raft's outboard motor was coughing and wheezing and chugging to a stop.

"Um, we sort of ran out of gas, too," Tommy glumly reported. "Sorry about that, you guys. Should've topped off the tank. It was on my to-do list. Actually, it still is..."

The dive boat drifted to a stop. The motor went quiet.

I could hear the waves slapping the sides of our rubber raft as the sea gently rocked us. Some kind of bird cawed overhead.

"How far are we from land?" Beck asked with a dry gulp.

"I have absolutely no idea," said Storm, looking up at the sun.

"Kind of wish we had our own helicopter," I said.

"Yeah," said Beck. "Me, too."

"Chya," said Tommy. "Our own helicopter would be cool."

Our dive boat was dead in the water.

And pretty soon, we might be, too.

CHAPTER 8

We drifted for more than an hour.

Make that two hours.

I knew this because my dive watch was still working, slowly counting down the remaining minutes in my life.

The blazing sun was unrelenting. There wasn't a cloud in the sky. And three of us were still in insulated rubber dive suits. I was so hot my sweat was sweating.

Tommy unzippered his front and slid in the laptop. "Don't want the salt water to compromise the chips and circuit boards and junk," he said, zipping back up.

"What about your sweat?" asked Storm. "It's salty, too."

"Maybe. But it's not as bad as the ocean. Trust me. I use a lot of body spray."

I turned to Beck.

"This could be the end," I said.

"I know," she said. Her lips were dry and chapped and flaky. "Sort of wish I'd grabbed Mom's lip balm instead of her jewelry..."

"Look!" shouted Tommy, popping up to his feet. "There. Off our starboard."

"What?" said Storm.

"A mermaid! She's come to rescue us!"

"You're delirious, Tommy. The sun is playing tricks on your eyes."

"No, it's not. That's a mermaid. See? She has long green hair and, uh, a very interesting tail..."

"That's seaweed clumped to a bumpy chunk of driftwood, Tommy."

Tommy sat back down. "Sure. Ruin my fantasy, Storm. Even though it's all I have left."

"Did any of you accidentally kill an albatross

recently?" asked Storm. "Because there's water, water everywhere and not a drop to drink."

Now Storm was becoming cuckoo. Reciting a line from "The Rime of the Ancient Mariner," a poem that Mom taught us in our homeschool English classes aboard *The Lost.* As I recall, the Rime had some pretty good rhymes in it. Wail and sail, mist and wist, weal and keel.

"Bick?" said Beck.

"Yeah, Beck."

"If this goes south..."

"Then we might end up in Egypt."

"No, I mean if this ends...horribly. If we die... well, I'm going to miss you. I think. I mean, maybe. I'm not one hundred percent sure."

"I might miss you, too, Beck."

"I might miss you more."

I shook my head. "No way."

"Way."

We would've launched into Twin Tirade number 2,043 if we'd had the energy. But the sun had drained all the fight out of us. We skipped ahead to the fizzle section of the tirade where we forget what we are mad about.

The sun was so bright and scorching I forgot a bunch of other stuff, too. Like my name. It had something to do with a pen, I think. What's a pen? I forgot that, too.

"I'm gonna close my eyes for a second," said Storm.

"No!" said Tommy, reaching out and shaking her. "If you close your eyes, you could sunburn your eyelids."

"I'm tired, Tommy. I'm also hungry."

"We all are," said Beck.

"I'll grab us some fish!" said Tommy, reaching into the water to swirl his hand around. "Ah, they're not biting…"

I sighed and closed my eyes, too.

And thought about how weird it was that Beck and I, twins who had been born on the same day, were also going to die on the same day and in the same rubber raft. I wondered if that could get us into *Guinness World Records*. That'd be cool.

Suddenly, something bumped into the bottom of our boat.

"What was that?" I shouted, totally startled. My eyes weren't closed anymore. In fact, they were kind of bugging out of my head.

"Probably a shark," said Storm with a shrug. "Here to put us out of our misery. Who wants to dive in first?"

Have I mentioned that Storm is the most morbid of my sibs?

Another bump. A big one. The whole raft wobbled. The shark was trying to burst our inflatable boat.

But the last bump was followed by a swirl of fizzy seawater just off our bow. A clear bubble emerged in the waves. A tiny woman was seated inside the bubble manning the computerized controls of what looked to be a surfacing submarine or giant version of one of those plastic balls you can buy in gumball machines. The woman wore eyeglasses with lenses thicker than the glass on the bottom of a soda bottle. Her chunky hair framed

her face. I recognized her immediately from our first trip to Egypt.

Aunt Bela Kilgore!

Mom's handler during her days as a spy with the CIA.

CHAPTER 9

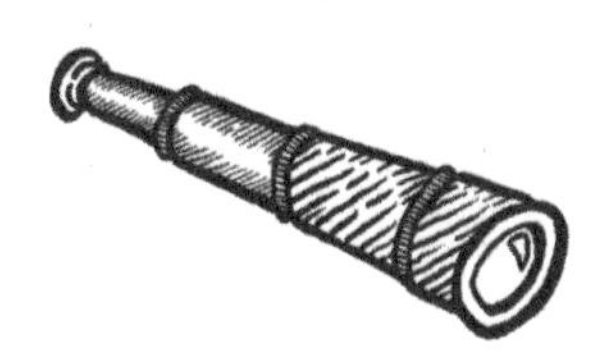

The first time we met Bela Kilgore was the last time we were in Egypt.

As you might remember, she blasted out of her twenty-second-floor Cairo hotel room window with a jetpack strapped to her back and crashed, headfirst, into the Nile river.

We'd thought she was dead. But, later, she resurfaced (literally) and helped us battle the evil Dionysus Streckting and the even-more-evil Uncle Timothy, who was *Dad's* handler at the CIA because Aunt Bela was a *double* double agent, who'd been working for Mom and Dad the whole time we thought she'd double-crossed them to work with Uncle Timothy, who really *was* a double agent pretending to be CIA while working for some super evil villains.

Phew.

The whole aunt/uncle/CIA thing was (and still is) extremely complicated.

Anyway, we were glad to have Aunt Bela pop up in the middle of the Mediterranean Sea because, if she hadn't, our current treasure-hunting adventure would've ended with our bleached bones floating around in a dinky rubber dinghy somewhere off the coast of Egypt.

"I thought you were your mother," said Aunt Bela, nodding toward Beck. "That pendant you're wearing is an official, government-issue DSED—Distress Signal–Emitting Device. Sue was supposed to turn it in when she left the CIA. Guess she wanted a souvenir. We suspect she also took a stapler and pad of sticky notes."

Now Aunt Bela turned to me.

"Ah! I see *you* have a brand-new Grecian urn."

"Yeah."

"It's very reminiscent of the one I airlifted

to Cyprus as a ransom payment to secure your mother's freedom from the pirates."

"Except," said Beck, "that one was priceless because it was *the* Grecian urn."

Storm, of course, gave us all the details on Grecian urn number one, even though we already knew them. "The very one the great English poet John Keats wrote about in his 1819 classic 'Ode on a Grecian Urn.'"

"This new one Bick's hugging cost sixteen dollars on Etsy," added Beck.

"Fifteen ninety-nine," I gently corrected her. "But it has great sentimental value. For me and for Dad."

"I'm certain it does," said Bela. "Bring it along. And hurry. Your raft is sinking."

Tommy twirled around. "Wha-hut?"

I looked down at my flippered feet. The sea was definitely rising around us and leaking through our not-so-inflated-anymore deck. Salty water was up to my ankles.

"I'm afraid I punctured your boat's bottom with my pointy-tipped antennae, which, of course,

I needed to track your distress signal. Also, on my rise to the surface, I noticed several sharks circling immediately below your vessel. They looked hungry. Climb aboard, everybody. Hurry!"

Storm clambered into the bubble-shaped submersible vessel first. Tommy went next because he was carrying the most precious cargo we'd hauled out of The Room: Mom and Dad's laptop. He still had it hidden under his wet suit. It's why his stomach looked even flatter than usual.

Beck and I went last.

And, yes, we sort of pushed and shoved each other during the whole boarding process. It's a twin thing.

"Batten down the hatches!" cried Bela. Then she punched a few buttons on her command panel. We heard servos whir and felt the cabin pressurize as all the curved glass panels locked into place. "Dive! Dive! Dive!"

For a small woman, Aunt Bela had a very big voice. Especially when it was sealed inside a reverberating glass bubble.

Aunt Bela pushed the control stick that made

her high-tech five-seater sub dive deeper. "I think it best that we slip into the port of Alexandria underwater so we can remain undetected by any reconnaissance aircraft."

"You mean like a helicopter or something?" said Tommy.

"Exactly. Your mother and father feared something like this might happen. It's why they asked me to be on standby and monitor my DSED scanner on a frequent basis. Usually, I just use it as a doorstop..."

"What do you mean they feared something like this might happen?" wondered Beck.

"Nefarious forces are at play, children," said Bela. "We're picking up chatter from some very bad actors willing to do whatever it takes to gain your parents' expertise, historical knowledge, and, apparently, some new form of technology they've developed."

"Oh," I said, "you mean the—"

Tommy, Beck, and Storm all shot me the same look. The one that silently screams, "Shut up, Bick!"

They were right. If our adventures had taught us anything it was that we couldn't trust anybody who wasn't part of our family—especially if they called themselves an aunt or an uncle. (Except, of course, Uncle Richie—but he was a *real* uncle, not the CIA code name variety.)

Bela was smiling at me. It crinkled her whole face. Made her look like a peach pit. "You were saying, Bick? What kind of new technology have your parents developed?"

"This cool new way to make a grilled cheese sandwich in the toaster oven."

Bela nodded. "I see."

"Chya," said Tommy. "You can totally understand why somebody would want to steal that. You don't need butter. It's, like, air-frying but without an air fryer."

We kept quiet and admired the underwater scenery for the rest of the ride. There were all sorts of pretty fish and swaying plants. I put my hands behind my head and leaned back in my comfy, cushy seat to study a school of sparkling striped fish scooting past our big underwater bubble.

Big mistake.

I had the Grecian urn on my lap. We hit some kind of underwater turbulence and the pot jostled.

Something clanged.

"Huh," I said. "There's something inside the urn."

Aunt Bela smiled over her shoulder at me. "Oh, really? What, pray tell, is it, Bickford?"

CHAPTER 10

I looked to Beck for guidance.

Yes, believe it or not, we both do that sometimes. Guess it's another twin thing.

Anyhow, I needed her take on our Aunt Bela situation. Remember, Aunt Bela used to be a spy. Maybe she still was. Let's just say I had my suspicions about her seemingly innocent question.

Beck gave me the quickest, smallest nod in the history of body language. Her nod said, "You might as well go ahead and tell her because she's not going to stop asking until you do, plus we'd all like to know what's hidden in that urn, too."

It was a very wordy nod.

So I unscrewed the squeaky lid of our souvenir Grecian urn, fished around inside, and pulled out its secret treasure.

A book.

"Aha," muttered Aunt Bela. "The third temple of King Solomon!"

"Excuse me?" said Storm. "The second temple in Jerusalem, the central place of Jewish worship, was destroyed by the Romans in the seventieth year of the common era. There is no *third* temple of King Solomon."

"You're right, Storm," said Aunt Bela, a little too fast and flustered for it to be the truth. "My bad. Had my numbers wrong. Second, third... almost said fourth. Hey, remember when you four went searching for King Solomon's Mines?"

Tommy, Bick, Storm, and I exchanged another patented Kidd family look. This one said, "She's babbling. Let it slide. We'll figure out the truth later."

I flipped through the first pages of the book. It was all about a flamboyant, fifteenth-century Gothic church called Rosslyn Chapel, located near Edinburgh, Scotland.

"Cool gargoyles," I muttered when I got to the section with a lot of pictures.

Aunt Bela looked up in the submarine's rear-view mirror (yeah, it had one) and smiled at me. Her cheeks crinkled into deep furrows. She could plant potatoes on that face. She really should use sunblock more often.

"One can assume that your father suspected you would grab that Grecian urn, eh, Bick?" she asked cheerily.

I shrugged. "Yeah. I guess. Just like Mom figured Beck would go for the pendant."

"As our parents," said Storm, "they have amassed detailed psychological profiles on all of us."

I think Storm was trying to change the subject—away from what we grabbed when we abandoned ship. We didn't trust Bela with any information about the item that Tommy took. The laptop. The one with all the data and the real technological advancement, the whole augmented reality mapping thing. The one zippered up against his abs.

"And what did you grab out of the room, Thomas?" asked Bela.

"A bag of chips," he said.

It wasn't so much a lie as an evasive maneuver.

Okay. It was a lie.

"But, well, when you're stranded in a raft surrounded by salt water, salty snacks sort of lose their appeal, know what I mean, Aunt Bela?"

He pulled a crumpled bag of crushed crumbs out of a side pocket in his dive suit.

"Hungry?"

She grinned. Politely. "No, thank you, Thomas. Sweet of you to offer."

CHAPTER 11

An hour later, the submarine whisked us into the Egyptian port city of Alexandria (founded in 331 BCE by a twenty-five-year-old Alexander the Great. Thank you, Storm).

After tying off at a dock filled with fishing boats, Aunt Bela took us to the Souk El Attarine, a maze of narrow alleys with all types of shops and stalls. We were looking for clothes because Beck, Tommy, and I needed something to wear besides our neoprene diving suits. My legs were super itchy after being wrapped up in rubber for so long. Storm grabbed a couple of new outfits,

DOES THIS OUTFIT MAKE ME LOOK TOTALLY AWESOME?

too. We also picked up small duffel bags to carry our gear.

Tommy had to practically peel the laptop off his stomach. It'd been sealed inside his suit for a long time. It was kind of glued in place. We rehid Mom and Dad's computer in the duffel, hiding it underneath all our diving equipment.

"This is my gift to you," said Aunt Bela with a broad smile. She paid for everything with a very shiny black credit card. "Now then, who's hungry?"

We all raised our hands.

Well, I only half raised mine. Because I noticed a very suspicious-looking man in a black suit and sunglasses spying on us from behind a stack of baskets in one of the stalls. Storm saw him, too. Not too many Egyptians were wearing dark business suits in the outdoor market.

"Friend of yours?" Storm asked Bela.

"No. I have absolutely no idea who he is..."

Beck and I exchanged yet another knowing glance.

Because we both knew Bela was lying.

CHAPTER 12

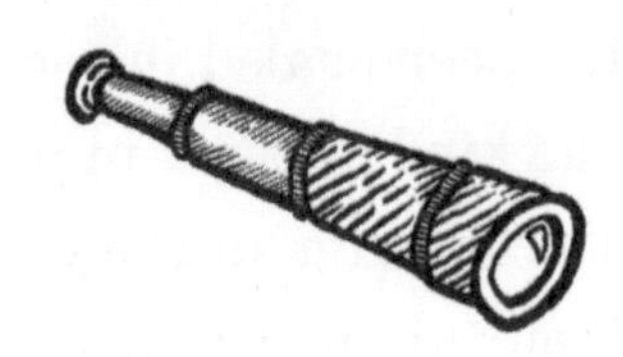

Our next stop was the Fish Market seafood restaurant, which had a spectacular view of the whole Royal Harbor combined with a pretty gross view of lots of fish and shrimp served with their heads still on and their buggy eyeballs peeping up at you.

I stuck to the hummus, tahini, and baba ghanoush with fresh-baked bread. Bread is always my favorite part of any meal. Especially soft and puffy pita bread.

Tommy, of course, was flirting with our server.

"So, what's on the menu?" he asked her. "Besides me 'n' u?"

She smiled a little. Bad move. Smiles only encouraged Tommy.

Or maybe she didn't really understand English and had no idea what Tommy meant. That happens with him. Even with people who speak English.

The food came and we started gobbling.

"Where are Mom and Dad?" asked Storm after she'd devoured a plate of prawns. "Who's after them this time?" (Good ol' Storm; she always gets right to the point.)

"Nefarious and evil actors," said Aunt Bela.

"Could you be a little more vague?" Beck asked sarcastically.

"I will answer your question with a question, Rebecca: have your parents recently discovered some kind of treasure in Scotland?" She flicked a fork in my general direction. "Perhaps something hidden inside the Rosslyn Chapel? Because that particular site has been linked to all sorts of long-lost treasures. Everything from the Knights Templar's gold to the Ark of the Covenant and the Holy Grail."

She got a wild, hungry look in her eyes and continued monologuing at us.

"Why, there are complex secret codes all over the chapel. Codes carved into the stonework and walls. Even the gargoyles tell coded stories. Children, if your mother and father found something, if they know how to crack those codes and unearth the hidden treasures of the Rosslyn Chapel, then somebody—perhaps somebody or some group that has been searching for that same treasure of treasures for a long, long time—may want to know what your mother and father know. They might've kidnapped your parents to force them to assist in a quest for riches beyond our wildest imaginings! One that has eluded treasure hunters for centuries."

I thought about what the lady in the helicopter had said to us through her bullhorn. She *did* want Mom and Dad to help her. She was planning on forcing their cooperation by threatening to hurt us. And there had to be a reason why Mom and Dad had hidden that particular book in the Grecian urn.

Now Aunt Bela's eyes widened out to full maniac.

"Why, this could be the greatest, most valuable, precious treasure that anyone has ever discovered! We'll be rich. Rich, I tell you! Filthy rich beyond our wildest dreams!"

I think she was about to let out a "mwa-ha-ha" when Storm arched an eyebrow. "We?"

Bela dabbed at her lips with a napkin and fumfered some more. "I meant *you*, of course. You and your parents. You'd want to share the treasure with your parents. At least until you turn twenty-one."

Aunt Bela checked her watch.

"Need to be somewhere?" asked Storm.

"No. Just like to be mindful of the time." She waved at our server. "Check, please!"

The beautiful server brought over our bill tucked inside a slender leather folder. Aunt Bela slid in her black credit card.

"Please bring that to me at the cashier stand whenever you're ready," said the pretty girl. Her English, by the way, was excellent. She winked at Tommy and waltzed away.

Tommy didn't have a cheesy comeback. Or a wink to give in return. In fact, he just sat there, staring out the plate-glass window at the Mediterranean Sea. He had the best seat at the table. The one with a panoramic view of the bay.

"Come on, guys," he said. "We should use the bathroom."

"All four of you?" asked a startled Aunt Bela. Then she glanced down at her watch. Again.

"Chya," said Tommy. "We were on that rubber raft for, like, a long time." He scooped up the slim binder with the black credit card jutting out up top. "I'll take this to the cashier stand on the way. We should probably take our bags, too."

"For goodness' sake, why?" asked Aunt Bela.

"Our parents taught us to be polite and never leave luggage where it could trip someone. Come on, guys. Now!"

Beck and I exchanged another look. This one said, "Why is Tommy in such a hurry for us all to go to the potty at the same time? And why are we taking our bags to the toilet?"

WE HATE TO EAT AND RUN, AUNT BELA, BUT... BUH-BYE. RUN, YOU GUYS. RUN!

But when we stood up from the table and grabbed our bags, we finally saw what Tommy had already seen.

A half dozen goons on jet skis zooming up to the docks below. Where they were met by a man in a black suit and sunglasses. The same sketchy dude who'd been eyeballing us at the souk. The man in the black suit made a sharp arm chop in our direction.

The goons were coming for us.

CHAPTER 13

"Wait!" shouted Aunt Bela. "Don't run!"

We did not take her suggestion. We ran faster! (Even toting all that gear!)

The pretty girl at the cash register made an amazingly gymnastic pommel horse move and flew over the checkout counter with a double leg swing. "Stop. Don't run! I think I love you, Tommy!"

Tommy didn't hesitate for even an instant. He kept running.

"How'd that girl know your name?" Beck wondered out loud.

“She has to be working with Aunt Bela,” said Tommy.

“No wonder her English is so good!” said Storm. “She’s a spy, too!”

We charged past a disgusting display of wide-eyed fish flopped on their sides in a bed of ice chips. They all looked like they were gasping for air, something I was also doing because Tommy was setting a pretty swift pace.

“Forget the girl!” said Tommy (for the first time ever). “Finding Mom and Dad is even more important than finding love!”

We slammed through the front doors of the restaurant, hit the porch, and dashed down the steep set of steps. In a flash, we were on the street.

“Wait!” shouted someone behind us. “We’re here to help!”

I figured it had to be the man in the black suit.

“Keep moving, Bick!” barked Storm. “You, too, Beck! They’re here to kidnap us the way they kidnapped Mom and Dad!” Storm was pumping her arms and chugging along like a freight train that just jumped its tracks because the rails were slowing her down. Our big sister could move when she wanted to. Right now, she definitely wanted to. She was only one stride behind Tommy.

"We need to find some place to hide!" I shouted as we darted down a side street and headed for an alley. We were practicing the evasive move techniques Mom and Dad had taught us, moves they'd learned in a CIA spy course called "How to Lose Your Tail." It wasn't about dogs, cats, or horses. It was about giving your pursuers the slip!

"How about that movie theater?" Tommy shouted over his shoulder.

Up ahead, on El-Gaish Road, I could see the marquee for the semi-shabby Abdel Moniem Gaber Cinema and Theater. From what I could make out from the vinyl banner stretched over the entrance, they were showing an action flick in 3D.

"Awesome!" said Beck.

She loves 3D movies. In fact, the last time Mom and Dad both went missing, Beck wore a pair of blue-and-red 3D glasses for months—long after the cardboard earpieces had gone limp and floppy on her.

"Tickets," said Storm between huffs and puffs. "Need. To. Buy. Tickets."

Without turning around, Tommy whipped up his left hand.

He held Aunt Bela's black credit card. He'd already been plotting this phase of our escape plan back when he offered to pay the cashier on our way to the bathroom. (See what I mean? Tommy is no dummy.)

We practically skidded to a stop outside the theater. I risked a glance behind us.

We'd lost the man in the black suit and his merry band of jet ski commandos. At least for now.

"No stopping for popcorn," Tommy said, hustling us into the dark and dingy theater.

"Actually," said Storm as Tommy paid for four tickets and four pairs of 3D glasses, "here in Egypt, crunching on pumpkin and sunflower seeds at the movies is much more popular than munching popcorn."

"Whatevs," said Beck, grabbing her ticket and 3D glasses.

"Come on," I said. "Let's go hide in a dark auditorium."

The theater was pretty empty. It was easy for us to find four seats together.

"Now what?" I whispered.

"We hope Aunt Bela can't track us down like she did last time," said Tommy.

And, the instant he said that, we all almost gave ourselves whiplash, twisting our heads to stare at Beck.

"Is that thing off?" I asked, nodding toward Mom's necklace pendant, which we all now knew to be an official, government-issue DSED—Distress Signal–Emitting Device.

"I think so," said Beck, fumbling with the teardrop-shaped fob.

"You think so?" I snapped.

"Well, Bick," Beck snapped back, "at least I'm capable of thinking."

Twin Tirade number 2,044 was hissed out in hushed bursts because screaming in a movie theater is considered rude. By the way, so is crinkling

the plastic wrapper on your candy box—except during a space battle scene with lots of explosions.

"I think you're going to set off that tracking device again!" I yelled under my breath, which is an extremely difficult thing to do, so give me points for that.

"It's not a tracking device!" said Beck.

"Is, too."

"Is not."

"So's your phone."

"Only if I have the GPS turned on."

"And do you?"

"Yes."

"Then turn it off!"

"Good idea, Beck," I said, starting my cooldown. "You should probably turn that thing off, too."

"Thanks, Bick," said Beck, also cooling off considerably. "Excellent suggestion."

Yes, just like the smooshed-together mound of squishy, creamy candy at the bottom of a jumbo-size box of Junior Mints, our anger was all gone before we knew it.

I turned off the location services on my phone.

Beck fidgeted with the pendant.

"Uh-oh," she said when, apparently, something she hadn't been expecting to happen happened anyhow.

"Did you activate it?" asked Storm, gripping both her armrests, ready to bolt out of the theater.

"No," said Beck. "But it popped open. There's something hidden inside!"

CHAPTER 14

"What is it?" I asked as Beck fumbled with the pendant that had turned itself into a locket filled with secrets. "Another book about that Scottish chapel?"

"No," she said, tilting back her 3D glasses and carefully extracting a folded-over square of paper, which she immediately started unfolding.

Tommy and Storm leaned in, too. We were all curious about what Beck had discovered tucked inside Mom's pendant.

"It's blurry," said Beck, squinting at the wrinkled rectangle. "It's printed in overlapping blue and red lines."

Storm's face lit up. And not just because she'd turned on the flashlight app in her phone to more closely examine Beck's slip of paper.

"It's an anaglyph!" she said with hushed excitement.

"Huh?" we all whispered back.

"An anaglyph is the stereoscopic 3D effect created by filtering each eye's image through different, usually chromatically opposite, colors, such as red and blue. When this anaglyph is viewed through color-coded glasses, the visual cortex of the brain blends the two separate images together into what it perceives to be a three-dimensional image."

We were all still staring at her.

"Huh?" I said it first.

"Put on your 3D glasses, Beck!" said Storm. "The image that Mom and Dad put on that slip of paper will fuse together in your brain."

Beck lowered her red-and-blue lenses. Then she gasped.

"It's a map. In 3D. The mouse type on the bottom labels it as the crypt beneath the Rosslyn Chapel."

"The one in Scotland?" I said, with a gasp of my own. "The one from the book hidden in the Grecian urn?"

"Uh, yeah," said Beck. "Duh."

"So, Mom and Dad definitely want us to go to this church in Scotland," said Tommy, rubbing his lantern jaw thoughtfully. "But why?"

Suddenly, someone swung a flashlight across our seats.

Was it the man in the black suit?

No. It was the usher.

"Kun hadyaa!" she said, giving us the universal index finger in the lips-shooshing sign. *"Ant tukhrib alfialam!"*

We didn't need to speak Arabic to know she was telling us to be quiet because we were ruining the movie for everybody else. I wanted to say, "Hey, the plot was doing that before we even sat down," but I don't speak Arabic.

CHAPTER 15

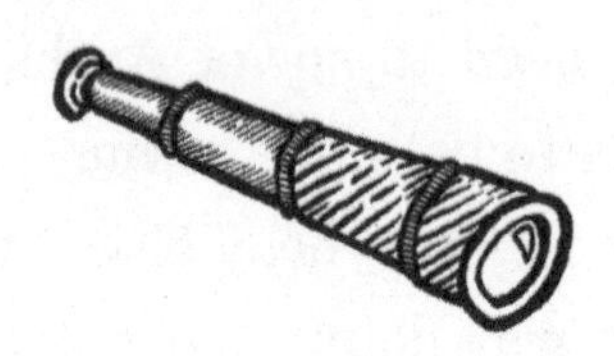

"Okay," said Beck, "clearly Mom and Dad were trying to tell us something about this Rosslyn Chapel in Scotland."

"Maybe it was the next treasure on their list!" I said. "Maybe we were going to go there to hunt for that world's-greatest-treasure-of-all-time dealio Aunt Bela was blabbing about."

"But then," said Storm, "somebody learned of their plans."

"Somebody bad," said Beck. "Somebody who had friends with a helicopter and a bullhorn."

"And," said Tommy, "those evildoers hijacked

Mom and Dad because they wanted to be filthy rich instead of us!"

"Actually," said Storm, "Mom and Dad would, most likely, turn over whatever they discovered in Scotland to the most appropriate museum or the treasure's original owners."

"Chya," said Tommy, sounding a little disappointed. "It's what they always do. Give the treasure away. It's why I'll never be able to afford a Lambo or a Ferrari."

"None of that matters," I said. "Mom and Dad are the most important treasure in the world."

"I don't say this very often," said Beck, "but Bick's right."

"Thanks, sis."

"He's also stinky, but that's not important."

"Not now," said Tommy. "But in Aunt Bela's sub? Whoa. Dude. Two words. Underarm deodorant."

"Isn't that three words?" I said, defensively.

"Nope," said Tommy. "Underarm sounds like two but it's actually one. Same with deodorant."

"Deodorant sounds like two words?" said Beck.

"Hey, it does to me."

"You guys?" said Storm. "We need to focus. Beck? Hand me that slip of paper. I'll memorize it. Front and back."

Beck handed Storm the tiny map of the chapel crypt.

"*Notas parere domina est scriptor*," said Storm.

"Huh?" said the rest of us.

"It's Latin. An inscription on the back of the map. It means 'Obey the lady's notes.'"

"What lady?" I wondered.

"Mom!" said Tommy. "She's the one who left us the note."

"I'm not so sure about that, Tommy," said Storm. "We need more information before we jump to any conclusions..."

"So, now what?" I asked.

"We destroy this evidence," said Storm. "We don't want Aunt Bela to know what we know even if we don't know exactly what it all means!"

"Um, why would Aunt Bela know about anything we're doing?" Beck wondered. "We just gave her and her goon squad the slip."

"Yeah," said Tommy. "Excellent evasive action, everybody."

"We also turned off all potential tracking devices," I reminded her.

Storm popped the slip of paper into her mouth as if it were a Skittle. She chewed a little and swallowed.

"Okay, guys, here's the plan. We need Aunt Bela. Because we need to fly to Scotland."

Tommy snapped his fingers. "And we can use Aunt Bela's credit card to buy airplane tickets or to rent a private jet like we did down in Australia!"

Storm shook her head. "No. Once she realizes that her credit card is missing, she'll cancel it. She's probably done that already."

"She also probably called the bank to report it stolen," I said.

"And to see if any charges have been made on it recently!" said Beck, completing my thought, because we twins do that sometimes, too.

"Those goons will be here any minute!" I said.

"Because I used her credit card to buy movie tickets!" said Tommy, slapping a palm to his forehead. "How could I have been so stupid?"

"Tommy," said Storm, "take it easy. What you really bought with Aunt Bela's credit card was time."

"And a chance to find Mom's hidden message!" I added. "Front and back."

"Which could only be read with 3D glasses," said Beck, "which you can only find in a movie theater."

"True," said Tommy, nodding and sounding way more pleased with himself than he had a few seconds ago. I guess that's what families do. We buck each other up when one of us is feeling down. "I did all that. I guess I'm so totally awesome that sometimes I don't even realize I'm being awesome, huh?"

Okay. Now he was just sounding obnoxious.

"So, what's the plan, Storm?" I asked.

She raised her hands over her head.

"To let Aunt Bela and her friends capture us," she said.

"And take us to Scotland!" I said half a second later. Because I'd finally figured out what Storm had been trying to say.

Half a second after that, the theater doors swung open.

Aunt Bela, the man in the black suit, and six goons in commando gear burst into the theater. The cashier from the restaurant was with them, too.

And they weren't there for the 3D action flick or the sunflower seeds.

CHAPTER 16

"So, we're not running away this time, right?" Tommy whispered out of the side of his mouth as Aunt Bela and the others marched down the aisle toward us.

"What?" I whispered back. "And give up our free ride to Scotland?"

"Go for it, Bick," said Beck and Storm, because they know I'm the family storyteller. I know how to "embellish" stuff. (And, yes, if a quick sketch could've worked instead, we all would've turned to Beck.)

"Okay, Aunt Bela," I said, channeling my inner

black-and-white mobster movie. "You nabbed us, you dirty rat. Sure, we thought we could outrun and outfox you but you outwitted us. You traced the credit card, didn't you?"

Aunt Bela smiled. "Yes. But only because I was concerned about you children."

"Me, too," said the man in the black suit as he whipped off his sunglasses dramatically. "We're from the United States government."

Now the cashier stepped forward and stood beside the man in black. "And we're here to help," she said.

"Hang on a second," said Tommy, with a hang-dog expression on his face. "Are you, like, with the dude in the suit? Is he your boyfriend, because, not for nothin', he looks to be like a decade or two older than you..."

"He's my boss," said the cashier, "not my boy-friend."

"Cool," said Tommy, regaining most (if not all) of his swagger. He held up both his wrists. "So, I surrender. You already have my heart. Take the rest of me. Please."

I'VE BEEN LEARNING ABOUT IMPORTANT DATES IN HISTORY. WANT TO BE ONE?

"Do you need to cuff me?" Tommy asked the cashier, wiggle-waggling his eyebrows.

"Hopefully that won't be necessary," said the man in the suit.

"It's not company policy when dealing with cooperative assets," added the cashier.

"Wait a second," I said. "Do you people work for the same company that Mom and Dad used to work for when Ms. Kilgore here was Mom's Aunt Bela?"

Beck rolled her eyes. "What my babbling brother meant to say was, 'Are you guys with the CIA?'"

Now every single member of the search party—the man in the suit, Aunt Bela, the cashier, and the six assorted goons—started looking from side to side and over their shoulders, all of them hoping nobody had heard what Beck had just said.

"Outside," said Suit Man. "Now."

Fortunately, the lobby was empty. Well, there were the four of us and the nine of them, but other than that the place was totally vacant.

A couple of the goons did that thrust-one-hand-in-the-pocket thing that meant that they either had a) concealed weapons or b) an awkward itch that needed scratching.

"We have a van waiting," said Aunt Bela. "It will take you four to a secure airfield. You need to be in Scotland, ASAP."

"Are you coming?" Tommy asked the cashier.

"Negative. My part of the mission is now complete."

"Bummer. Oh, by the way—I seem to have lost my phone number. Can I have yours?"

"Into the van, Thomas!" barked Aunt Bela. "Now."

The four of us were, more or less, hustled into a van with very darkly tinted windows. The thing looked like Darth Vader on wheels. Black Suit and Aunt Bela, along with two of the goons, climbed in with us. Our gear was stowed in the rear cargo area.

The cashier, much to Tailspin Tommy's dismay, hopped on a motorcycle with another goon and sped away—probably to break some other "asset's" heart the way she'd just broken our big brother's.

"Allow me to officially introduce myself," said

the man in the suit who was riding in the back of the van with us. One of the goons was at the wheel. Aunt Bela was also up front, riding shotgun. Another goon had the last row of van seats all to himself. They basically had us surrounded.

The man in the black suit kept up his introduction. "You four can call me Uncle Sam."

"Clever," I said. "Because you work for the United States government. Uncle Sam..."

"No. Because my name is Samuel Heenehan and I will be your direct contact and liaison with the intelligence community as we initiate active measures to secure the return of our missing assets, a.k.a. Dr. and Mrs. Kidd."

"In other words, you're our handler?" said Storm, cutting through all the bureaucratic gibberish. "And you're going to help us rescue Mom and Dad."

"Roger that," said Uncle Sam. "Locating your parents is priority one of this operation."

"And what, exactly, is this operation?"

Aunt Bela swiveled around in her seat up front.

"The clues your parents left you confirm what we suspected. They anticipated their kidnapping by those who would use their treasure-hunting skills and knowledge for purely greedy purposes. We need to rescue your mother and father and stop the bad guys. We need to be in Scotland at the third temple of King Solomon!"

Storm exhaled mightily. "Aunt Bela? We already discussed this. There is no third temple of—"

Uncle Sam held up a hand to cut her off.

"It's what some people call the Rosslyn Chapel in Scotland," he said.

"Really?" said Tommy. "Why? I mean the place already has a perfectly good name. 'Rosslyn Chapel.' Sure, the Third Temple of King Solomon is snappier, catchier—"

Now Uncle Sam cut Tommy off, too.

"Many call it that because they suspect that's where the Knights Templar hid their vast treasure," he explained. "The treasure they collected over many years guarding the site of that second temple of King Solomon in the Holy Land during the Crusades."

"And," said Aunt Bela, her eyes sparkling, "as I may have mentioned, if the Knights Templar treasure is, indeed, hidden inside the Rosslyn Chapel, we're about to recover the biggest, hugest, most gigantically extraordinary treasure in the history of the world!"

CHAPTER 17

Aunt Bela, once again, forgot to mention the biggest, hugest, most extraordinarily important treasures of this current quest.

Mom and Dad.

She seemed to be all about the gold, jewels, and ancient artifacts. On the other hand, *we* wanted to put our family back together. And it sure looked like (based on the clues Mom and Dad must've known we'd find) we needed to be in Scotland to get it done.

So we played along.

In about an hour, our van reached what had to be a secret CIA airfield in the middle of the desert. Sand was swirling up into dust devils. A sleek private jet was parked on the runway with its stairway door open and down.

"That's our ride, Kidds," said Uncle Sam. "We need to be Oscar Mike—on the move!"

Someone in a flight suit and mirrored aviator glasses slid open the side door of the van and we all tumbled out.

"This is where I leave you!" said Aunt Bela, shouting to be heard over the drone of the private jet's twirling turbines. "You're in good hands with Uncle Sam."

Beck and I exchanged a glance. Every time somebody called the agent in the black suit "Uncle Sam," we pictured an angry old guy with a stringy white goatee and a star-studded Yankee Doodle top hat pointing at us and screaming, "I WANT YOU!"

Well, we wanted this Uncle Sam, too. No, we *needed* him. Because everybody seemed to think that whoever sank our ship had also hauled our parents off to Scotland for a quick Knights Templar treasure quest. And Uncle Sam was our only ticket to Scotland. We had no other way of getting there. (I did mention that our ship had sunk, right?)

Mr. Heenehan, or Uncle Sam, took the first row of seats. The four of us found two rows of seats facing each other across a small table near the rear of the cabin. There were, of course, a pilot and copilot up front in the cockpit. There were also four CIA agents spread throughout the plane. They all had bulges in various parts of their clothes, depending on where they stowed their weapons.

We had an eight-hour flight ahead of us.

So, Storm, our walking Wikipedia, launched into a brief historical recap of the Knights Templar. A real data dump.

"They were formed in 1120 during the Crusades in what was called the Holy Land. The knights' official name was 'The Poor Fellow-Soldiers of Christ and of the Temple of Solomon.' Temple Mount in Jerusalem was their headquarters for the next sixty-seven years. They made money guarding roads and protecting pilgrims.

They were also supported by contributions from extremely wealthy families. Lots of people also think the knights found some kind of super buried treasure during their time in Jerusalem. That would help explain how they became so fabulously wealthy so fast."

"They were in that movie, too!" I said. "*National Treasure.*"

Beck gave me an eye roll. "That was a made-up story, Bick."

"Hey, those are my favorite kind."

"Anyway," said Storm, trying to get back to her historical info drop, "ninety percent of these so-called knights weren't fighters or even monks. They were what we'd call bankers. Some say they had more than a billion dollars' worth of gold, silver, and royal crown jewels."

"So, how'd their treasure end up in Scotland?" I asked.

"The Crusades crumbled in the thirteenth century," said Storm. "The Templars had to abandon Jerusalem. They fled to France. But when King Philip took the throne, he didn't like the Templars. In 1307, he even sent his army to raid the Templar headquarters in Paris. It was a fortress, with thick walls and sturdy towers, built to protect all the gold, silver, and jewels hidden inside. But the Templars' treasure vaults were empty. Someone had snuck off with all the loot. Maybe a knight who rented a ship or two, crossed the English Channel, and sailed north to Scotland to hide it all again."

"In a chapel, instead of a fort!" said Beck.

Storm nodded. "Exactly."

"Mom and Dad must've found the secret hiding spot!" I blurted.

"No wonder the bad guys kidnapped them!" added Tommy. "I know I would've if I were, you know, a bad guy looking for a quick and easy way to dig up a bajillion dollars' worth of medieval-style treasure."

That's when Uncle Sam came walking up the aircraft's aisle with what looked like a secure satellite phone pressed tight against his ear. He was crushing it against his face the way some people do because they think it will, somehow, improve their reception.

"Can you hear me now? How about now? Good, good."

He seemed oblivious to the fact that, in addition to whoever was on the other end of the call, the four of us could hear every word of his conversation.

"Tell the team at State to relax. We're making terrific progress. Our friends should be very pleased very soon. With the help of Dr. and Mrs. Kidd, we *will* recover their treasure for them. I guarantee it."

The four of us exchanged a worried glance.

Earlier, Uncle Sam had said that locating our parents was "priority one of this operation."

But what if priority one was just the first step toward the real priority, which maybe they called priority two: recovering the treasure for the CIA and State Department's friends?

What if those "friends" weren't so friendly?

What if Uncle Sam and the whole intelligence community was actually working with the same people who'd kidnapped Mom and Dad?

CHAPTER 18

When we landed in Scotland at the Edinburgh Airport I was not, no matter what Beck might tell you, tempted to buy a kilt at the Tartan Weaving shop.

My knees are too knobby to wear a skirt.

As we hurried through the concourse carrying our small duffels, I swear I heard somebody blowing a bagpipe. Either that or a goat was sick.

Uncle Sam and his team had arranged a caravan of three identical black SUVs to motorcade us from the airport to the town of Rosslyn, about seven miles south of Edinburgh, which, in case Storm hasn't told *you* yet, is the capital of Scotland

and has been since at least the fifteenth century.

Not that any of us asked, but Storm also taught us some more Rosslyn Chapel history. But she had to do it in bite-size chunks. The CIA driver had his pedal to the metal and we probably traveled those seven miles in under five minutes. (I think Storm's backseat history lesson had encouraged the guy to drive even faster than spies usually drive; we're talking "getaway vehicle" speed.)

"Chapel founded in 1446," Storm blurted. "By William St. Clair. Third and final St. Clair prince. Long history. One St. Clair fought at the Battle of Hastings. William the Conqueror was his cousin. Some St. Clairs are now named Sinclair."

"Like the ones who run the gas stations," said Tommy, nodding thoughtfully. "I dig their dinosaur, Dino..."

"Wasn't Dino on *The Flintstones*?" I said.

"No," said Beck. "Dino is a South Korean dancer and a member of the boy band Seventeen."

Yes, sometimes when Storm tries to teach us stuff, we try to throw her off track.

It never works.

"Five centuries after they started construction," Storm continued, "the chapel's still not finished. Lots of stonework. Carvings. Stone angels playing instruments. A hundred pagan Green Men on the walls. Sculptures of the Seven Deadly Sins dancing across an arch. Also—"

"And here we are," said the driver, slamming on the brakes and screeching to a halt.

"Lots of tourists typically visit," said Storm, who could just keep going and going. "The Rosslyn Chapel has been in books. Movies. Both. *The Da Vinci Code...*"

Uncle Sam, who'd been in the lead car, was already out of his vehicle and raring to go. He yanked open the door closest to Storm.

That finally flicked her off switch.

"Our local asset has arrived," Uncle Sam reported. "Her name is Fiona Glendenning. She's a college student, working on her doctorate in history. Ms. Glendenning knows more about the Rosslyn Chapel than just about anybody."

Storm huffed a little at that. "That remains to be seen," she muttered.

Uncle Sam must not have heard Storm because he kept going. “She also knows a great deal about the Knights Templar.”

Storm gave that an eye roll. “As do other people.”

“It’s something of a personal passion with Fiona.” Uncle Sam gestured toward a woman with blazing red hair standing in front of the welcome center entrance. “She’s eager to help us find what we’re looking for.”

"Whoa," said Tommy as the woman began walking toward us. "And I'm eager to help her find what she's looking for, if what she's looking for is love."

Yep. Not even a full day after falling in love in Egypt, Tommy was doing it again in Scotland.

CHAPTER 19

While Tommy chased after the new girl of his dreams, Storm stared up at the chapel's Gothic pinnacles, flying buttresses, pointed arches, and other architectural stuff used in cathedrals that Mom taught us about when we had our Middle Ages unit on board *The Lost*.

"All right, Kidd Family Treasure Hunters," said Uncle Sam, "let's go inside and hunt some treasure!"

Storm nodded. "We need to find the treasure before Mom and Dad's kidnappers do. Otherwise?" She made a slicing gesture across her throat. "As

THIS IS AMAZING!
HA! WHY DIDN'T YOU SAY THAT WHEN I CARVED A DUCK OUT OF A BAR OF SOAP?

soon as they have the Templars' treasure, they won't keep Mom and Dad alive."

Storm: Unlike coffee makers, she has no filter.

We all entered the chapel.

"Whoa," said Tommy as he and Fiona stared up at all the gewgaws and gargoyles. Almost every inch of the walls, pillars, arches—everything—was covered with intricate carvings. It reminded me of a Christmas tree with way too many ornaments.

Fiona was showing Tommy all the stone angels playing a dozen different musical instruments, including one blowing bagpipes.

"You're the only angel I see," Tommy told her, earning his first Fiona groan.

Storm started giving us the guided tour Fiona thought *she* was supposed to give. "Some people think the carved cubes protruding from the arches over the section known as the Lady Chapel create a secret code with their thirteen different geometric patterns—a code that spells out the notes to a musical melody."

"It's true," said Fiona. "The key to that secret

melody is right there in that angel. The one holding a musical staff and pointing to the A, B, and C notes."

Storm gasped. Very loudly. It was almost like a backward burp.

"*Notas parere domina est scriptor!*" she shouted.

"Huh?" said Fiona.

"Is that still Latin?" I asked. "Because I forget what it means."

"'Obey the lady's notes,'" said Storm, translating. "And this is the *Lady* Chapel. Fiona—has anyone ever recorded the melody the blocks spell out on the ceiling?"

"Aye. I have a recording of it right here on my phone."

"Perfect. We're going to need it. Downstairs. In the crypt."

"Why?"

"Because, like I said, we need to 'obey the lady's notes'!"

CHAPTER 20

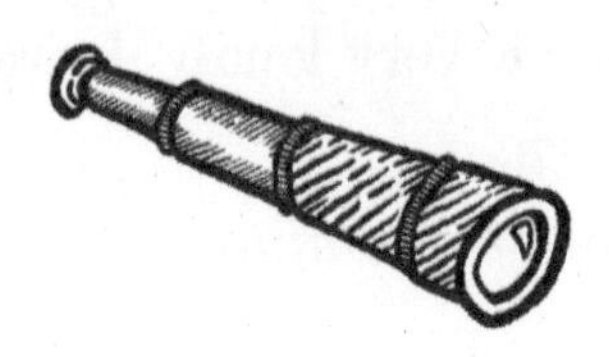

"Let's head downstairs," said Uncle Sam, echoing Storm's command. "We have an all-access pass."

"For real?" said Tommy. "How'd we score that?"

Uncle Sam whipped off his aviator shades and gave Tommy a stonier look than any on the faces of the chiseled stone carvings.

"We have our means and methods, son," was all he said.

I looked around. We were the only ones in the chapel, which was supposed to be a big tourist attraction. They even had a gift shop and cafe, both of which, come to think of it, were completely empty when we arrived. Obviously, the CIA's means and methods weren't just about buying up all the tickets.

"Follow me." Storm, who had obviously memorized the chapel's floor plan, led the way over to a steep flight of stone steps heading down into an underground chamber.

"I thought I was supposed to be the tour guide," I heard Fiona mumble.

"Sorry," said Tommy. "If Storm's on the tour, you don't stand a chance. But I could use a little guidance on my personal journey, because I'm getting lost in your eyes."

Fiona actually chuckled at that one.

The temperature seemed to drop ten degrees as we plodded down the steps into the dank chamber below. Cold wrapped around us like a blanket, even though most blankets are, you know, warm.

"About twenty of Rosslyn's barons were buried under the chapel in subterranean vaults," said Fiona before Storm could. "But those tombs were sealed up long ago. No one knows where the entrance is."

She turned to look at Storm. Just in case.

"Correct," said Storm. "But I do know that this crypt we're standing in is the oldest part of the chapel. This space was used as a workshop while the masons and stone carvers were working upstairs."

"What's that marking on the wall?" asked Beck. She was pointing to a spot right beside an arch in a side wall.

"Ah," said Fiona. "People used to think that mysterious carving was a stonemason's template for the pinnacles up on the roof."

"Nope," said Storm. "The angles don't match."

Whoa. Guess she memorized those, too. And she didn't even pack her protractor.

"However," Storm continued, "the angles and arrangement of the carving seem to match up perfectly with an ancient Viking sea chart that Mom and Dad shared with me when I was, oh, about three, maybe four."

Now Fiona's jaw was hanging open. "You read Viking sea charts when you were a child?"

Storm shrugged. "I found them to be more fun than picture books. Anyway, this map would lead you to the discoveries the Vikings made in North America, long before Christopher Columbus bumped into the Bahamas on his way to India."

"Fascinating," said Fiona. "I did not know that. Probably because my parents didn't give me maps to read when I was a wee lass. They mostly drilled me in...other things. Like horse-riding."

"Storm's awesome on a horse, too," I said.

Fiona sighed and threw up her arms in surrender. "I'm sure she is."

"Too bad that Viking map on the wall can't tell us how to find the Templar treasure," said Tommy.

Storm grinned. "Maybe it can. Fiona? How about a little music? Please place your phone's speakers up against the wall there."

Fiona looked confused. "You want me to play music for a carving in a stone wall?"

Storm nodded. "Yep. If we 'obey the lady's notes,' I think this old Viking map might lead us to a new world filled with riches."

"Play the music, Ms. Glendenning," barked Uncle Sam. "Play it now!"

CHAPTER 21

Fiona placed the speaker end of her phone up against the cold stone wall. She pressed Play.

Out came the sound of a beautiful angelic choir. If heaven has a Spotify channel, this tune is probably on it.

"The thirteen notes," said Fiona. "In the key indicated by the angel holding the musical notes. We call it the Rosslyn Motet."

Before she could say another word, the stone with the Viking map started to shimmy and shake. It was quivering its way forward. Pulling itself out of the wall.

"Sympathetic resonance," said Storm. "That single stone has been tuned to the music's frequency and is responding to the external vibrations of your motet. It's the same principle often demonstrated by a tuning fork."

Storm whipped out her phone, slid her fingers across the glass, and opened an app to record the music pouring out of Fiona's phone.

About a minute later, Uncle Sam blurted, "And what the heck is a motet?"

"A short piece of sacred choral music," Storm and Fiona said at the same time. "Vocals only," added Storm. "No instruments."

"It's a wee bit like medieval a cappella music," said Fiona.

While Storm and Fiona conducted their quick music appreciation class, the stone wobbled halfway out of the wall, exposing chiseled handholds on either side.

"Come on, Mr. Heenehan," Tommy said to Uncle Sam. "It's 'heave-ho' time."

They each grabbed hold of one of the recessed nooks and yanked the tall block forward. They tugged and the rectangular slab slid all the way out like a piece in a giant Jenga puzzle. It also floated a quarter of an inch above the floor so it wouldn't leave any scrape marks and give away the secret stone's hiding place.

"Whoever designed and engineered this stone doorway sure knew what they were doing," said Beck with a great deal of admiration for her fellow artistes.

"They were expert masons," said Fiona. "They could make stone do almost anything."

“Well,” said Tommy, snapping on a flashlight and ducking down to enter the secret passageway. “Let’s go see if they knew how to make this particular stone hide a bajillion dollars’ worth of treasure!”

CHAPTER 22

As we made our way through the narrow tunnel, we quickly discovered where some of those twenty dead Rosslyn barons were buried.

In vaults built into the sides of the sloping shaft we were traveling through.

There wasn't much left of the dearly departed royals. Just a

THIS IS WHERE BICK WANTS TO SOUVENIR SHOP?

bunch of bones, dust, and tattered clothes. One or two helmets. And a shield. The shield was pretty cool.

Every ten feet or so we'd come upon another buried baron tucked into the wall for their final nap. There were so many skeletons, it felt like we were walking through one of those Halloween pop-up shops.

Since people were shorter back in the olden days, we weren't actually walking. The curved stone ceiling of the passageway was only about four feet tall so even Beck and I had to hunch down to avoid bumping our heads. And the air kept getting chillier. We were definitely descending deeper beneath the chapel.

"We're doing this treasure hunt to find our parents," I heard Tommy tell Fiona. "And if we don't find them, we'll be orphans again."

"You can be an orphan more than once?" said Fiona.

"Chya. In our family, anyhow. Mom and Dad keep disappearing on us..."

"My parents have also disappeared," said

Fiona, sadness making her voice catch in her throat.

"Whoa. Seriously? You're a potential orphan, too?"

"Yes, Tommy. We have that in common."

"Plus the fact that we're both extremely good looking."

"I would do anything to get my parents back," Fiona said, wiping away a sniffle. "Anything in the world."

"Do you see anything up there, Tommy?" asked Uncle Sam, who was bringing up the rear.

"Yeah," said Tommy, sounding wistful. "A sad and beautiful redheaded girl who misses her mom and dad. Just like me. Not that I miss her parents. I never even met them, so..."

"What about the treasure?" said Storm, who was behind me and Beck.

"Hang on," said Tommy. "It looks like this tunnel ends in another chamber. Could be another crypt."

"Could be the treasure room!" added Fiona. Her sniffles, tears, and sadness were all gone.

Potential treasure will do that to you.

When Beck and I tumbled into the chamber behind Tommy and Fiona, they were already swinging their flashlights up and down and all over the damp stone walls.

"No treasure," said Tommy, sounding totally bummed.

"No fresh carvings, either," said Fiona.

She pulled out her phone and hit the Play button. The Rosslyn Chapel motet choir reverberated off the walls.

Nothing happened. No part of the walls was tuned to sympathetically resonate with the choir's vocals.

"No magic dancing blocks of stone," said Tommy. "It looks like a dead end."

"What about that?" said Beck, swinging her flashlight across the floor.

She'd seen something!

CHAPTER 23

"Check it out, you guys," said Beck, the dusty beam of her light spotlighting the even dustier floor.

There were footprints stamped into the dust at the far end of the room.

"Have you been back to that section of the chamber, Thomas?" asked Uncle Sam.

"Nope. We were kind of looking for Viking maps down at this end first."

"This is as far as we ventured before you lot came in behind us," added Fiona.

"That means somebody else has been in this room!" I blurted.

"Exactly!" said Beck.

"Way to go, sis!"

"Thanks, bro!"

"Hang on, everybody," said Storm. "Don't move!"

And then, *she* moved! She totally disobeyed herself. She dropped down on all fours and slowly made her way past Tommy and Fiona.

"Um, Storm?" said Tommy. "What're you doing? You kind of look like a bear."

"I need to examine these prints," she said, shuffling forward. "The tread pattern of the foot-wear."

"Uh, why?" I asked. "We didn't come down here to shoe shop."

"She's doing forensic analysis of the available evidence," said Uncle Sam. "Just like your parents would."

"Oh. Right. My bad."

"It's a match," Storm announced.

"With what?" asked Fiona.

"My shoe impression database." She tapped the side of her head. "This is definitely the tread

pattern of a size eleven-and-a-half D pair of Dunham Captain Limited men's boat shoes. It's all dad ever wears on board *The Lost*."

"Dad was here?" I shouted it so loud, my voice rang back to me off the walls.

"Yep," said Storm. "Mom, too."

"Mom was here?" screamed Beck. Her voice was even sharper, pinging back off the stone.

Storm's headlamp bobbed up and down when she nodded. "Yep." She pointed to another footprint in the dust. "Those are her Chuck Taylors."

"So they already grabbed the treasure?" grumbled Uncle Sam.

Storm stood up and dusted off her pants, which were covered with a thin film of gray, ashy powder. "Mr. Heenehan?" she said, sounding a lot like Mom does when she's disappointed in an answer we give on a pop quiz.

"Yes, Ms. Kidd?"

Storm swept out her hand. "Do you see that part of the floor where there are no footprints?"

"Yes. Of course I do."

"Does it look like Mom, Dad, and their kidnappers dragged and pulled treasure chests and all sorts of ancient artifacts across it? Do you see skid marks? A cluster of footprints? Or does it look like a drabber, dustier, grimier version of the Sahara desert?"

Uncle Sam looked slightly embarrassed. "Desert," was his almost-silent reply.

"So that means," said Tommy, snapping his

fingers because he just figured it out, "Mom and Dad were here, but the Knights Templar treasure wasn't."

Uncle Sam nodded. "Clever. It was your father and mother's attempt to buy us some time to catch up with them."

"And to drop us a clue!" I shouted, because while everybody else had been yabbering and deducing junk, I'd been swinging my flashlight around on the floor. The beam glimmered when it hit something gold tucked into a nook at the farthest corner of the room.

We all scurried over to see what it was.

"It's the edge of a coin!" said Fiona.

A coin that someone had kicked into a tight crevice where the stone wall met the stone floor.

"Pry it out!" cried Beck.

"On it," said Tommy, finding just the right tool on his always handy Swiss Army knife.

"Careful," said Fiona. "Try not to scratch it. It could be a rare artifact."

"Don't worry," said Tommy. "I'm a trained professional treasure hunter. I've extracted more gold from tight places than most dentists."

Tommy eased the coin out of its snug slot.

Fiona, just as carefully, plucked the gold piece off the floor.

"Okay," said Fiona. "On one side we have a Knights Templar cross."

"You sure about that?" asked Uncle Sam.

"Trust me," said Fiona. "That's what it is. On the flip side...I'm not sure. It's an engraving of a fort? Maybe a castle?"

"Mind if I take a look?" said Storm.

"Be my guest." Fiona passed the gold coin to Storm.

"Interesting. It appears to be the Château de Gisors. In France."

Fiona gasped. "You're right. That's where the Knights Templar were once imprisoned!"

"I know," said Storm. "And, I suspect, that's where Mom and Dad are headed next!"

"They left us a bread crumb to follow!" said Beck.

"I love when they do that!" said Tommy.

"We need to be in France," said Uncle Sam. "Yesterday!"

CHAPTER 24

Uncle Sam organized a pretty impressive ride from Scotland to France for us.

This time, I am talking about the United States government and not the CIA guy, Sam Heenehan. Because we hitched a ride in an AWACS. That's what the US Air Force calls its Airborne Warning and Control Systems. It's like a flying, high-tech command center.

"We have drones with eyes in the sky over the Château de Gisors, sir," reported one of the military techs manning a joystick and studying overhead footage of the castle. "No sign of Dr. or Mrs. Kidd. Or any hostiles."

"Roger that," said Uncle Sam, who was kind of strutting around all the computer workstations filling up the cargo hull. "How are we doing with the facial recognition software?" he asked an officer, who was clicking her mouse like crazy.

"We had a hit on them. Yesterday. In the Normandy area."

"The Château de Gisors was a key fortress for the dukes of Normandy in the eleventh and twelfth centuries," said Storm.

We all said, "Shhh!" to her because we were trying to eavesdrop on Uncle Sam.

"Where were they?" he asked the tech.

"A small bakery called the Boulangerie Rivière, sir. They both pop up on the behind-the-counter security camera. In fact, Mrs. Kidd winks directly at the lens."

"Mom," Beck and I said with a sigh. Our mother is pretty awesome.

"Anyone with them?" Uncle Sam asked the computer lady.

"Affirmative, sir. A man and a woman. Both are unknown to us or to Interpol. Fascinating."

"What?"

"Taking another look at the bakery footage. Dr. Kidd is holding a baguette. Then he tears off the top. Finally, he drops the crumbs to the floor."

Tommy, Storm, Beck, and I turned and smiled at one another.

"What?" said Fiona. "What's going on?"

"Dad," I told her. "He's leaving us more bread crumbs."

"Confirming we're heading in the right direction," added Storm.

"Chya," said Tommy. "Dad and Mom are way better at this stuff than Hansel and Gretel."

Beck and I stood up to stretch our legs while Tommy and Fiona drifted off to a quiet corner of the cargo hold. Storm stayed where she was, flipping through a six-inch-thick binder. I think she was memorizing a flight manual. Either that, or she wanted to figure out how to operate the humongous radar dish on the back of the AWACS's fuselage.

"Hey, Beck?" I said.

"Yeah."

TAP TAP TAP
I WONDER IF THESE THINGS HAVE ANY VIDEO GAMES ON THEM.
I WANT THE RADAR DISH TO DO THE FOUR-DAY WEATHER FORECAST.

"Don't you think this is a little much?"

"Huh?"

"It seems the government's throwing the full weight and might of the United States military into a missing person search."

"So? You don't think Mom and Dad deserve the best?"

"Of course I do. It's just that..."

"What?"

"I don't know. Something's fishy about all this."

"No, Bick. You're just smelling things. Have you changed your underpants lately?"

Beck shook her head and walked away. She was probably right. I was probably overthinking things, which isn't something I usually do. I'm more of an under-thinker. So, to shake the suspicious thoughts out of my head, I drifted over to where Tommy was chatting up Fiona.

"That's so sad," I heard Tommy tell her. "Your parents abandoned you?"

Fiona nodded. "It was four years ago. They fell in with the wrong crowd. I guess you could call it a cult."

"Whoa. Cults stink. One time, in the rain forests of South America, where we were searching for the Lost City of Gold, the high priest of a seriously weird cult was all set to sacrifice me to their god. It involved removing my heart while it was still beating. Fortunately, my brother and sisters got me out of that mess."

"I don't have any brothers or sisters."

"Oh," Tommy said. "Family can be annoying sometimes. Like when they squeeze the toothpaste from the *middle* of the tube. But they can also be the coolest thing in the whole wide world. The greatest treasure of them all."

"I wish I had family like that."

Tommy wiggle-waggled his eyebrows. "Don't worry. I'll share mine with you. But first, we need to put it back together. We need to find Mom and Dad!"

CHAPTER 25

It was kind of late when we arrived in the small town of Gisors, France.

"Still no movement up at the castle," said Uncle Sam as we checked into the Château Hôtel des Écuries, which was only eight minutes away from the other château—the castle that would be the next stop on our treasure quest.

The hotel was pretty grand. Like a fancy country home set at the end of a long pebble driveway. There was a restaurant off the lobby that looked pretty popular with the locals, many of whom were sipping wine, nibbling cheese, and saying "*mon Dieu*" because, hello, they were French.

There were also horse stables. In fact, that's what *écuries* means.

Uncle Sam handed out keys. Tommy and I would share a room on the second floor. So would Storm and Beck. Fiona would be on the third floor, bunking with one of the female CIA agents in our crew of six.

"We'll depart for the castle first thing tomorrow morning," Uncle Sam told us. "Oh-seven-hundred hours. Grab a croissant before you hop into the van. We won't have time to stop for breakfast. Our intel suggests that your parents and their kidnappers are also in this same general vicinity. We need to find the castle's treasure and haul it out before they show up to try and do the same."

"Haul it out?" I said.

"Shouldn't we just hide behind it and wait till the bad guys show up?" said Beck, hopping onto my train of thought as it chugged through her brain. It's a twin thing.

"That way, we could nab the kidnappers," I said.

"And rescue Mom and Dad," said Beck.

"Once we have them..."

"Our mission is complete."

"You arrest the kidnappers..."

"Mom and Dad tell us what to do with the treasure."

"It's simple."

"Easy peasy."

Uncle Sam's head was swinging back and forth like he was watching a ping-pong match, trying to keep up with us. I thought he might give himself whiplash.

"Negative!" he finally shouted. "We need to control the treasure to control the kidnappers. Grab some dinner, then grab some shut-eye. Tomorrow promises to be a busy day."

Beck and I headed up to our rooms to dump our stuff. Well, our one duffel bag each.

We were both kind of starving, so we hurried back down to the lobby and hit the restaurant, hoping to enjoy some of that famous French cuisine. Or we could just suck on a stick of butter, which would basically taste the same.

Storm was already in the restaurant. "The

escargot is delicious," she told us. "If you like snails swimming in garlic."

All of a sudden, Beck and I weren't so hungry. We ordered bread. It was long, crusty, and chewy. Like I said, no matter the cuisine, bread is always the best part of any meal.

We heard familiar laughter out in the lobby.

Tommy.

Storm slurped down her last snail, and Beck and I brushed the bread crumbs off our shirts. The three of us hightailed it into the lobby to see what all the laughter was about.

"This is amazing, Tommy!" said Fiona.

She was wearing one of our augmented reality diving masks and was moving her arms around as if she were swimming. Tommy was sitting in a nearby chair, Dad's laptop open and running in his lap.

"It would be even cooler if you were actually diving off the coast of Egypt," Tommy told her. "Then that ancient temple you're swimming around in would be, like, superimposed over what's actually there now, which is mostly sand and murky water. And fish. There were some very pretty fish."

"It's like you can see into the past!" said Fiona, peeling off the dive mask. "All the way to ancient Egypt."

"Exactly," said Tommy. "It's how I found this really awesome statue of Cleopatra on our last dive."

"*Excusez-moi, s'il vous plaît,*" said a French man wearing a white turtleneck under a corduroy blazer. He was also wearing a beret. Like I said, he was French. "If you do not mind telling me, what is this goggle device you two are utilizing?"

Tommy was about to tell him.

But Storm stormed in. "Nothing. A silly computer game. A mere toy. *Un simple jouet.*"

"*Oui?*" said the man.

"Oui en effet!"

"Ah," said the man, who was wearing leather gloves and puffing on a pipe suspiciously. "I had hoped, from what they were saying, that it was, how you say, something more? Something *extraordinaire.*"

"Sorry to disappoint you," I said. "It's just a video game. About fish."

"It's *Finding Nemo,*" said Beck.

"Right. From the movie."

"Yeah," said Tommy, finally catching on. "We were playing *Finding Nemo.*"

Fiona shrugged. "I never saw the movie."

"It's from Pixar," I said. "Good stuff. Lots of fish. Very colorful."

"Ah," said the man. "In that case, so sorry to disturb. Please, enjoy your Nemo gaming device." He gave us a slight tip of his beret. *"Bonne nuit. Au revoir."*

"So long!" said Storm, waving buh-bye to the man who slowly stalked his way across the lobby. He had long legs like a stork.

When he was finally out the door, Storm, Beck, and I whirled around on Tommy.

"My bad," he said.

"Why are you trying to find this Nemo?" asked Fiona.

"It doesn't matter," said Tommy, closing the laptop. "From now on, all I'm focused on is Finding Mom and Dad!"

CHAPTER 26

"Family meeting," said Storm. "Upstairs." She nodded toward Beck. "Our room."

"Can Fiona join us?" asked Tommy, raising his eyebrows like an innocent puppy.

"Is she family?" asked Beck.

"Not yet," said Tommy with a sly grin. "But I'm working on it."

Fiona laughed. "That's okay. You four have a lot to discuss. And, if all goes well, you'll be reunited with your parents tomorrow. I, on the other hand..."

Her lips went from smile to quiver in a flash. Tears welled up in her eyes. She sniffled and snuffled. I figured she was, once again, thinking about how her parents had abandoned her. How her family, unlike ours, would never be reunited.

She bolted for the elevator. We let her go. We wanted to give her a private moment with her grief. Plus, there's nothing worse than riding in a cramped European-style elevator cage with someone who's weeping. Those things are tiny.

A few minutes later, when the four of us were in Beck and Storm's room with the door locked, Storm asked Tommy if he had done any serious work on Dad's laptop.

"You mean like a spreadsheet or something? Maybe a PowerPoint presentation?"

"No!" said Storm. "Like searching through Dad's files."

"Well," said Tommy with a wink. "Fiona's been keeping me kind of busy."

Storm grabbed the laptop and opened it.

"See anything?" I asked.

"Yep," said Storm. She tapped the screen and a file labeled "srosiG ed uaetâhC."

"Oh, it's one of those Google-generated secure passwords," said Beck. "I hate those things."

I agreed. "Me, too. How could anybody remember that string of hooey?"

"Chya," said Tommy. "It looks like some kind of secret code."

"Oh, it's code, all right," said Storm. "The simplest code in the universe. It's Château de Gisors spelled backward."

"Ohhhh," said Tommy. "Clever. You'd need, like, a mirror to decipher it."

"Riiight," said Storm, clicking the file open.

"Oh, yeah," said Tommy, as we all clustered behind Storm to peer over her shoulders at the screen. "Mom and Dad were chasing down that Templar treasure, big-time!"

The file was filled with images of the Château de Gisors castle with its octagonal tower and forbidding walls.

"It was built by the Normans in the twelfth century," said Storm.

"Weird coincidence," said Tommy. "Everybody on the construction crew was named Norman?"

"The Normans were a people, Tommy," said Storm. "They were related to the Norse Viking settlers of this region of France. The Normans actually ruled England during the time the château was being built."

Now Storm pulled up another image.

Of a dungeon.

There was a caption underneath it.

Storm read what Dad or Mom had written: "In 1312, the Knights Templar, once the superheroes of the Crusades, were outlawed by the Pope and the King of France. They were rounded up and imprisoned all across the countryside. Their assets were seized."

I picked up the narration because I can do dramatic readings way better than Storm and things were about to get gruesome.

"Some of the Templars ended up in the dungeon at Château de Gisors, where they were tortured into confessing crimes they hadn't committed and then executed for those same trumped-up charges. One of the knights imprisoned within Gisors's walls was Jacques de Molay, the last Templar grand master."

Tommy whistled. "The big cheese. If anybody

would know where the Templars hid their treasure, it'd be the grand master."

"Totally," I said.

Storm finished reading the caption. "They were miserable, sick, and starving."

"Get this, you guys!" I said, skipping to Mom and Dad's final note. "During their time in the prison beneath the Château de Gisors, the captured knights carved some very strange and interesting graffiti on the dungeon's stone walls."

"We need to see that graffiti!" said Tommy.

"First thing tomorrow morning," said Storm. "And, Tommy?"

"Yeah?"

"From now on, please guard this laptop with your life!"

CHAPTER 27

It was just after dawn when we climbed into a blunt-nosed minibus with Uncle Sam and two other CIA agents.

The CIA team was wearing clothes that made them look like American tourists. There was a lot of plaid, polo shirts, safari vests, and dad jeans.

Tommy was lugging a backpack.

"It's got the laptop in it," he whispered to us. "I'm not letting this thing out of my sight again!"

And then he tossed it into the empty row behind him. Where, of course, he couldn't see it.

"Tommy?" said Storm. She nodded her head toward the backpack.

"Oh. Right."

He reached around, grabbed the knapsack, and placed it on his lap.

The minibus rumbled down the pebble driveway, heading for our hotel's gated exit. It'd be an eight-mile drive up to the castle.

"Tommy?" said Fiona, who was sitting beside him. "I want to apologize for my emotional outburst yesterday."

"Hey, that's okay. I totally understand. Your parents abandoned you. That's gotta hurt. But maybe you should try to move on. Remember—refusing to let it go is kind of like hugging a cactus. The tighter you hold on, the more it's going to hurt."

"I guess..."

"At least our parents never abandoned us," I said proudly.

"Uh, yes, they did," said Beck.

"Uh, no," I told her. "They never have and they never will."

"Oh, really? How about when Dad"—she made air quotes—"'disappeared'?"

"That wasn't the same as abandoning us," I insisted. "He disappeared on us."

"By hopping on a helicopter in the middle of a tropical storm!"

"He had to do that!"

"Well, maybe Fiona's parents had to do what they had to do!"

Yep. Right there, in the back of the bus, with three CIA agents gawking at us, we launched into Twin Tirade number 2,045. According to the dictionary, tirades (originally a French word, by the way) are supposed to be long, angry speeches filled with furious criticism and snarky accusations. Our Bick and Beck Twin Tirades, however, were typically short. Like sparklers that set off a shower of sizzling sparks but quickly fizzle into a glowing red stick before cooling completely into a crisp twig of black soot.

"Dad didn't abandon us!" I yelled.

"Did, too!"

PLUS CHIANT QUE TOI, TU POURRAS PAS EN TROUVER!*
@%#
WHEN DID YOU LEARN FRENCH?
I DIDN'T.
WHAT? YOU JUST INSULTED ME IN FRENCH.
BECAUSE IT'S SO EASY TO DO IN ANY LANGUAGE!
CHATEAU DE GISORS
SIGH...
*IT'S NOT POSSIBLE TO FIND SOMEONE MORE ANNOYING THAN YOU!

"It's not abandonment if he planned on coming back!"

"Oh, really? How could he be so sure he could come back?"

"How could you be so stubborn?"

"How could you be so stinky?"

"Easy. I didn't take a shower this morning."

"Neither did I!"

"Because we're both in a hurry to find Mom and Dad."

"Exactly," said Beck. "We can't abandon them to whatever fate the pirates who sank *The Lost* might be planning for them!"

"Of course we can't!" I said.

"Because *they* would never abandon *us*!" said Beck.

"Agreed."

"So, why are we yelling?"

"I forget."

"Me, too. Are you gonna finish that croissant?"

"Nope. You can have it. There's chocolate in the middle."

"Nom, nom, nom."

"Yeah. Delish."

And just like that, we were done.

The bus was silent.

Until one of the CIA agent's radios startled to cackle. She touched her earpiece.

"Sir?" she said to Uncle Sam.

"Yes, Agent Catino?"

"Our drone operators just made another pass over Château de Gisors. They say there's a welcome party waiting for us at the castle."

"A welcome party?"

"A group of what appear to be medieval reenactors. They're all dressed up in suits of armor and carrying pikes and banners. Apparently, they look like they're ready to march to the Holy Land and join the Crusades."

"Which," muttered Storm, "ended in 1291 when one of the only remaining Crusader cities, Acre, in what was then known as Palestine, fell to the Mamluks."

"So, why is this crew all dressed up?" I wondered.

"Maybe they're the French version of the Civil War reenactors at Gettysburg," said Tommy.

"Maybe they're just a little early with their Halloween costumes," said Beck.

"Or maybe they belong to a cult," mumbled Fiona.

There was only one way to find out. We had to get off the bus and see what these knights were doing up so early in the morning.

CHAPTER 28

"Huzzah!" shouted a knight in shining armor as we disembarked from the bus.

He had on a helmet and what Storm told me later was a white surcoat and mantle, both with red crosses emblazoned on them. I would've called the surcoat a dress, because it had a skirt. The mantle? That would be the blouse. The guy was also gripping a flapping white banner that sported another one of those red crosses. All of them were shaped like the one we'd seen on that coin back in Scotland.

"That's the Templar cross," Storm reminded us as we sized up the dozen medieval reenactors standing in a loose formation in front of the Château de Gisors. Several of the knights playing dress-up wore helmets that resembled buckets with only an eye slit. Others had hoodies made out of little linked chains. They all carried swords and shields. Their gloves, what Storm called gauntlets, were shimmering steel. They were the kind of gloves that wouldn't be much good in a snowstorm. They'd rust.

"To what do we owe the honor of this welcome?" asked Uncle Sam, stepping forward to address the leader of the group.

"We like to give a special greeting to all our VIP tourist guests," said the man toting the Templar flag. "Would you like to pose for a souvenir photograph?"

"Negative," said Uncle Sam, who, by the way, looked pretty ridiculous in his tourist disguise: Hawaiian shirt, bright-blue shorts, bulging camera bag, and sideways baseball cap, which was an even brighter blue than his shorts.

Tommy looked like a typical college kid with a backpack. So far, he was keeping his promise. The hidden laptop was staying with him at all times.

"We only ask you for a small donation," the part-time Templar told Uncle Sam. "Five euros." He gestured toward Tommy, Storm, Beck, and me. "Perhaps something with just the children?"

"Fine," said Uncle Sam, digging into his shorts to find the cash and handing it to the head knight. "Kidd family? Pose pronto. We need to be Oscar Mike."

"On the move!" said Tommy, proud that he'd picked up some CIA lingo.

"Roger that. By the way—what's in the backpack, Thomas?"

"Dry socks," said Tommy, without skipping a beat. "Wet ones make my feet itch."

"I see," said Uncle Sam, not sounding like he totally believed Tommy's answer. "Hustle in for the snapshot, Kidds. The sooner we're finished out here, the sooner we can take care of our business inside."

The four of us bustled over to where the knights were waiting for us. Beck, Tommy, Storm, and I stood together. The knights clustered around us.

Uncle Sam held up his phone and we all said "fromage," which is French for "cheese."

Suddenly, just as Uncle Sam snapped our picture, a sleek black helicopter rose up over the tree line.

It was that lady, the one someone called Dame Elizabeth, the same wackaloon who tried to sink our rubber raft with her rocket launcher. This time, she didn't want to blow anything up. She just leaned out of the side of her chopper with her long-lensed camera and whir-clicked through a burst of photographs. Then the helicopter zoomed away.

"What's she doing here?" said Storm.

"Being weird," said Beck.

"Yeah. Who is she?" I wondered out loud. "Some kind of flying paparazzi?"

"Why is she here in France?" said Storm, her face scrunched in thought.

"Fiona?" said Tommy, running over to where the newest love of his life stood frozen, staring up at the sky with her mouth hanging open. "Are you okay? Fiona?"

"No," she said with a shiver. "It couldn't be."

"It couldn't be what?" said Tommy.

"Never mind. My eyes are playing tricks on me. I'm seeing things."

"What kind of things? Puffy clouds that look like bunny rabbits? Because you're still staring up at the sky where the helicopter used to be."

Meanwhile, Storm still had that very worried look on her face.

"Storm?" I whispered. "What's wrong?"

"Why did that lady from the helicopter in the Mediterranean Sea snap another 'proof of life' photo of us?"

"Probably to prove to Mom and Dad that we're still alive," said Beck. "Probably to threaten to hurt us if Mom and Dad don't hurry up and find the treasure."

"We need to be down in the dungeon!" I reminded everybody.

"*Oui*," said the French guy posing with the fluttering banner. "For you are all enemies of the Knights Templar!"

And that's when we heard the unmistakable THWICK-CLINK sound of steel swords being pulled out of scabbards.

That's when the fake knights who'd greeted us became super real!

CHAPTER 29

"*Voilà!*" proclaimed the head knight. "That *final* photograph was all we needed to prove to your parents that you remain in our custody!"

"Final photograph?" said Beck.

"As in, the last one we'll ever pose for?" I asked.

"*Oui!* Kidd children? We no longer need you alive. This photograph will convince your parents that you are now our prisoners. Therefore, prepare to meet your maker!" His sword glinted in the sun as he swung it up to his side.

The other eleven not-really-reenactors raised their weapons, too.

"*Deus vult!*" the knights shouted as they clanked and clunked in a line toward us.

"That's the Crusaders' battle cry," said Storm, because, well, she's Storm. "It's Latin for 'God wills it.'"

"No, He, She, or They do *not* will it!" said Tommy, assuming a martial arts ready stance.

"Tommy?" said Beck. "You can't karate chop a sword! You'll lose a finger!"

"Or a whole hand," I added.

"We're not karate chopping anything," said Uncle Sam.

He and his two fellow CIA agents pulled out their semiautomatic sidearms and opened fire.

But the knights were like heavily armored tanks. The bullets just pinged and dinged off their shiny metal breastplates.

"Well, you definitely dented them good," said Storm sarcastically, as we all backed up. "They may kill us, but at least they won't be getting back their damage deposits on those costumes!"

Soon, the slowly moving line of heavily armored knights came close enough to swing their pikes and staffs and send the CIA agents' weapons skittering across the castle's parking lot.

"We're defenseless!" shrieked Fiona.

"Oh, no, we're not," said Storm. "To the battering ram!"

"The what?" I shouted.

"The bus!"

"Excellent suggestion!" shouted Tommy. "Come on, everybody! This time, I'm driving!"

We all ran as fast as we could to our parked minibus. Since we were in shorts and running shoes, we could travel a whole lot faster than the twelve knights lumbering around in their heavy metal leggings and cast-iron clodhoppers. They were moving like a squadron of Frankenstein monsters. One clunky step at a time.

In a flash, we were all on board the bus.

"Buckle up," said Tommy as he slipped behind the wheel, hunching forward because he was still wearing his backpack. "I have a feeling we're gonna hit a few speed bumps." He cranked the ignition and loudly revved the engine a few times to warn our attackers what their fate would be if they didn't retreat. The knights froze.

"Run away!" I heard the muffled voice of the lead knight cry out. "Run away."

"Help!" shouted another. "We need air support! Radio in air support!"

"Air support is only a last resort!"

"Call it in, sire. Call it in!"

Air support? I thought. What do these knights think this is? Some kind of alternative history game where the Knights Templar command an air force squadron?

The clanging, clattering, clinking crew slooooowly turned around just as Tommy slipped the bus into gear.

They weren't moving very fast.

We were! I knew Tommy wouldn't really mow them down, but he'd definitely make them run around in circles and work up an exhausting sweat inside their tin cans.

Just then, another helicopter appeared on the horizon.

A big cargo kind of craft. A troop transport!

There was a masked man in one of the windows

NOW THIS IS WHAT I CALL DEFENSIVE DRIVING!
EEEK!

aiming another rocket launcher at us.

Tommy slammed on the brakes. We screeched to a stop.

"Stay where you are, Kidds!" came a voice over the chopper's loudspeakers. "And don't even think about shooting down our aircraft with your drones, government agents."

I glanced over at Uncle Sam. He was talking into his sleeve. Was he calling in our own air-strike?

"Dr. and Mrs. Kidd are on board with us!" boomed the loudspeaker.

WHAT?!?!

I couldn't believe it. Mom and Dad were on the helicopter?

Impossible! But then Dad stepped into the open cargo door. It looked as if his hands were tied behind his back. A masked thug in a flight suit was holding Dad roughly by the shoulder with one hand while his other hand aimed a pistol at his head. Another masked goon jammed a microphone in Dad's face.

"Don't worry about us, kids," said Dad. "Your

Mom and I are fine. So, when you're down, just focus on what's important and ignore everything else. We'll all be together again soon. I promise!"

"Enough," grunted the goon holding the microphone. He pulled it away from Dad and put it up to his own mouth. "Knights Templar? It is time to evacuate! Now!"

The chopper touched down. The guy with the rocket launcher kept it trained on our bus. Tommy raised his hands above the steering wheel to let the missile shooter know he wasn't going to try anything cute or funny. The twelve knights staggered toward the cargo door and clambered aboard.

"We should do something!" said Beck.

"We can't," said Uncle Sam. "They have that rocket aimed at us."

"It's a stalemate," I said. "Neither side can win. If they blow us up, Mom and Dad will stop helping them track down the treasure. But we can't blow them up once they're airborne or we'll be shooting down Mom and Dad, too."

There was nothing we could do.

So we just sat there and watched the knights shamble their way on board the helicopter. One by one. Except the last guy, a knight with a bucket helmet. He slipped and toppled backward, landing upside down like a tipped-over turtle.

No one hopped out of the helicopter to help him.

No one even seemed to care that he was stranded on the ground.

The side door slid shut.

The chopper lifted off.

And turtle man kept kicking his legs, flailing his arms, banging his bucket head, and trying to roll over in his heavy steel shell.

CHAPTER 30

We were in a good news/bad news situation.

The good news was that we now had our own "proof of life." Dad and Mom were alive!

The bad news? They were still kidnapped and in grave danger—bouncing around in the belly of a cargo chopper with a bunch of medieval maniacs!

Also, I had a feeling their kidnappers were (with Mom and Dad's forced help) a step or two ahead of us in the whole Templar treasure quest thing. I figured the bad guys had already been inside the Château de Gisors and had picked up whatever secrets might be hidden inside its stone walls and turrets.

But, like Dad said, we needed to focus on the important stuff. We could still salvage the most valuable treasure in the world: our family. We just had to keep finding and working the clues!

Still stunned from seeing Dad, we all were just kind of standing there, watching the chopper lift off.

Fiona was in a daze again, too. "It can't be…" she muttered.

"What?" Tommy asked.

"It's nothing. My ears are playing tricks on me."

"Seriously? Earlier it was your eyes. Now it's your ears?"

Fiona nodded.

Tommy looked concerned. "Are you sure you're getting enough sleep? Eating your vegetables?"

"I think so…"

"You guys?" I said, noticing that Uncle Sam and the two other CIA agents were already standing beside the sprawled-on-his-back bucket head knight. "We need to be over there. We need to hear what Bucket Head tells Uncle Sam!"

"Totally!" said Tommy. He led the charge across the grassy field, his backpack bouncing and slapping his spine the whole way.

"They abandoned me?" we heard the knight moan in despair when we joined the three CIA agents hovering over him. His voice sounded even sadder echoing around inside his trash basket of a helmet. It also didn't sound French. More like he'd flown to France from New York to join the cause.

KNIGHT HAS DEFINITELY FALLEN. AND CAN'T GET UP.

Was this some kind of international conspiracy?

"Yo, abandoning someone in distress is completely against the official code of chivalry," whined Bucket Head. "Where was their gallantry, huh? How dare they forsake me in my hour or, you know, minute of need? That's against all the Knights Templar rules!"

"Let's help him up and get that helmet off his head," said Uncle Sam.

"Chya," said Tommy, bending down to lend a hand.

"You could move more freely if you slipped off that knapsack, Thomas."

"No, thanks."

Tommy and the CIA team carefully eased the knight into a standing position. Then they helped him remove his helmet.

As the tight coffee-can-ish headgear squeaked up over his ears, it revealed a bright-red Knights Templar cross tattooed beneath the guy's left eye.

"He's in the cult!" gasped Fiona. "The new Knights Templar."

"Is that a thing?" asked Beck.

Fiona nodded. "Aye. It surely is. I've been doing research on them at college!"

"What's you name?" Uncle Sam asked the fallen knight.

"Knight Rodrigo," the man replied. "Used to be Bob. Bob DeBartolo. From Brooklyn."

"Well, Knight Rodrigo, we'd like to have a little chat with you."

"Verily. I shalt speaketh true."

"Um, you guys?" I said. "Did everybody forget why we came here in the first place? To look for a clue."

"Which," said Beck, "the bad guys might already have."

"Oh, they do," said Knight Rodrigo. "I didn't hear what it was; just that they found it downstairs in the dungeon."

He nodded toward the castle looming over us on its hill.

We all kind of stared at him. Bad guys usually don't give up information like that so quickly.

"Dude," said Tommy. "Where'd you go to henchman training school? You're not supposed to spill the beans like that."

Rodrigo shrugged. "Unfortunately, it's another part of the whole code of chivalry thing. We must always speak the truth. 'Whether in honor or disgrace, a knight must always make his report with the greatest fidelity to the facts. Thou shalt never lie.'"

"Noble," I said.

"But not very practical if you're gonna be in the treasure-stealing business," added Beck.

The knight nodded. "Tell me about it. But, you join a club, you read the rule book, and you follow it."

"We need to go check out that dungeon," Storm said to Uncle Sam. "Immediately. If we can find the clue that Mom and Dad already found, we might be able to catch the kidnappers before they get too far away and do something horrible to our parents."

"From what I hear," said Knight Rodrigo, "the plan is to burn them at the stake as soon as the treasure is ours. That's what the King of France did to a bunch of the original Templar big shots. Sorry. Gosh-darn chivalry code. Gotta tell you the truth, no matter if it stings, know what I mean?"

"You Kidds go find the clue," said Uncle Sam. "My two colleagues and I will talk to Mister Rodrigo—"

The Templar politely raised his index finger. "*Knight* Rodrigo."

"Whatever," said Uncle Sam. "We'll learn what we can from him. You learn what you can from that castle!"

CHAPTER 31

Tommy and Fiona decided to stay with Uncle Sam and the rest of the CIA team while they questioned Knight Rodrigo.

That was a smart move. As you might've guessed, none of us totally trusted anybody whose first name was Uncle or Aunt. We'd been there, been burnt by that.

So, it was just Beck, Storm, and I bounding up the hill to dash into the Château de Gisors. We followed the signs directing us down a curving set of stone steps to the dungeon.

We reached the bottom of the staircase and stepped into the cold, dark prison where so many

Knights Templar were once held, including Jacques de Molay, their last grand master.

"Wait a second," said Storm as we stepped into the cylindrical cell where the walls were covered with ancient, chiseled graffiti. "Dad wasn't giving us a pep talk when he was in that helicopter."

"Really?" I said. "You didn't find it inspirational when he said that whole bit about 'when you're down, just focus on what's important and ignore everything else'?"

"I did," said Beck. "I might even put it on a T-shirt, even though it's kind of long. I'd have to use the front and the back..."

"You guys?" said Storm. "It was a clue. 'When you're down' meant when we came down here to the dungeon!" She gestured to the walls, which, like I said, were completely covered with all sorts of chiseled images. "Now we need to focus on what's important and ignore everything else."

"Seriously?" said Beck. "There are so many weird shapes carved into these walls."

"We have to find the important ones," said Storm, "and ignore all the others."

I nodded. "I guess when you're a prisoner, there isn't much to do besides swill gruel and scratch stuff on the walls."

"Fascinating," said Storm.

"What?" Beck and I said at the same time.

"There. On the southeast wall. Do you see it? The image of a treasure chest, a bear, the cross—which is actually five different crosses and commonly referred to as a Jerusalem cross—and a castle?"

"Yeah," I said.

"I guess," said Beck.

Storm kept going. "The Jerusalem cross, of course, is another symbol from the Crusades."

"Of course," we both said, even though we had no idea what Storm was talking about.

"The treasure chest," said Storm, tapping it lightly, "has to be a reference to the Templar treasure."

"What about the bear?" I asked.

"The bear is the heraldic symbol you'd put on a coat of arms to symbolize protection."

"And the castle?" asked Beck.

"The fortress protecting the treasure," said Storm.

"So what?" I said. "That last grand master of the Knights Templar scratched this into the wall to let his troops know their treasure was safe and protected in a castle somewhere in the Holy Land?"

"Exactly," said Storm. "Well done, Bick."

"Thanks. I think."

"But where is this castle?" asked Beck. "There were probably a bunch in the Holy Land during the crusades."

Storm leaned in and closely examined the etching of the walled fortress. "The shape of this castle seems vaguely familiar."

Now she raised her eyeline and stared at the Jerusalem cross.

"Of course!" she said. "It's the key. The focal point. The precise spot where we need to do like Dad said and focus."

She pulled out her phone and called up the compass app. "The center of the cross at the center of the other crosses gives me a southeasterly coordinate of 135 degrees."

Storm tapped her phone's screen and called up a map pinpointing our current location near Gisors, France. "We are here," she said. "If I plot a straight line on a bearing of one hundred and thirty-five degrees, it takes me south and east across Europe, over the Mediterranean Sea, straight to the Holy Land, also known as modern-day Israel, and—yes, of course!"

"Um, of course what?" I wondered.

Storm tapped the map. "Here. On the coast. The town of Acre. The last stronghold of the Knights Templar. Remember? The place where the Crusades ended in 1291 when the castle fell to the Mamluks. The imprisoned grand master was telling a secret to those he knew would come after him. The Templar treasure is still there! In Acre, Israel!"

PART TWO

THE KIDD FAMILY CRUSADE

CHAPTER 32

We came out of the castle with our new intelligence and went over to share it with Tommy, Fiona, and the CIA guys.

We were going to need the CIA's help to travel from France to Israel. We still didn't have a boat, a car, or a plane of our own.

The CIA team, along with Tommy and Fiona, were still listening to Knight Rodrigo, who sure liked to talk. Even while chomping on a gooey croque monsieur, which is a ham-and-melted-cheese sandwich. (By the way, "croque monsieur" roughly translates into "Mister Crunchy," who, I guess, is a distant French cousin to Mister Softee, the American ice cream guy with the swirl cone head.) Apparently, Uncle Sam had decided to play "good cop" with the abandoned knight and feed him lunch. So we decided to listen to what the fallen knight had to say before we revealed any of the new information we'd picked up down in the dungeon.

"The plan was to kidnap the finest treasure hunters in the world to help us, you know, hunt the treasure," the former bucket head said, his mouth full of bread, ham, and chewy cheese. He also had some kind of creamy sauce dribbling down his chin. "We thought about nabbing that guy Nathan Collier from TV."

"Collier!" said Tommy, pounding a fist into his open palm the way he did whenever somebody mentioned that name.

For years, Nathan Collier had been our parents' number one nemesis. He has a sleazy TV show on a skeevy basic cable channel. (I think it's called the Underwater Weirdo Network.)

"But we did our homework," said Rodrigo. "Collier just follows you Kidds around the globe and steals your glory. So, our fearless leaders,

Knight Hugo and Dame Elizabeth, suggested we go after your mother and father. We traced you to Egypt. Stormed your vessel. Captured your mom and pops. Sank your ship and doctored a few photographs to convince your parents that you four were in our custody."

He showed us a photograph. One that didn't obey that chivalrous code of ethics because it was a total lie. Fake news! Our rubber raft was never surrounded by a fleet of knights on jet skis. The hems of their robes would've been soaked. If

they'd really zoomed across the salty water of the Mediterranean Sea like that, their armored joints would've been rusted tighter than the Tin Man's in *The Wizard of Oz*.

"Who exactly are this Knight Hugo and Dame Elizabeth?" asked Uncle Sam.

"They're the brains behind this whole operation. They realized we should reclaim what is rightfully ours, because, come on..." He tapped the red cross tattoo under his eyeball. "We're the new Knights Templar and we've got the tattoos to prove it. Any treasure the original dudes plundered back in the day, technically, belongs to us now because we're following all their rules. Even the one prohibiting pointy shoes and shoelaces. And since the Templar treasure is worth bajillions, we could use that money to buy some shiny new armor and snazzy new flags. We could also start our own cable network—Templar TV. Hey, this treasure is so humongous, we could basically rule the world."

Uncle Sam leaned in. "Tell us more about this Knight Hugo and Dame Elizabeth."

Rodrigo crunched into his sandwich a little deeper. "They're the big cheeses. Of course, having a Dame Elizabeth is, you know, a modern twist. The original Knights Templar didn't allow women in their club. Heck, you couldn't even hug or kiss a girl."

Tommy shook his head. "Barbarians," he muttered.

Me? I would've been fine with that particular rule. Who needs gross stuff like hugging and kissing?

"Back in the Crusades," Rodrigo continued, "a Knight Templar couldn't even take a bath without getting permission from his superior officer. Then there was that whole vow of poverty thing. You weren't allowed to carry cash. Also, you couldn't play board games. Chess was against the rules."

"So, what part of the Knights Templar vows did you people keep?" asked Storm.

"The costumes. And the swords. I like the swords. And the treasure. We're all pretty excited about finding the Templar treasure."

"I assume Hugo and Elizabeth are aliases," said Uncle Sam. He nodded to one of the other agents who opened up a white paper sack. The deliciously oily aroma of french fries tickled my nose. "What are their real names?"

"We have pommes frites," said the agent holding the bag with the grease-speckled bottom. "Very thin. Very crispy."

Rodrigo licked his lips. "They're Scots. From Scotland."

Fiona gasped.

"Their real names are Callum and Amelia."

Fiona gasped again.

"Callum and Amelia Glendenning."

Fiona gasped one last time. A really deep one. I thought she was going to faint. Her face turned bright pink. Her ears burned so bright, they disappeared in her red hair.

"I knew it!" she said.

"Cool," said Tommy. "Um, what did you know?"

"I wasn't seeing or hearing things," she said. "That was my mother, Amelia Glendenning, in the first helicopter with the long-lensed camera. And that masked man with the microphone was my father, Callum Glendenning!"

"Whoa," said Beck. "Wait a second. Your parents kidnapped our parents?"

"Your parents sank our ship?" said Storm.

All Fiona could do was nod and sigh, "Aye. It seems they truly did."

CHAPTER 33

Uncle Sam's CIA helpers transported Knight Rodrigo to a "secret detention facility" they sometimes used in France.

The rest of us headed back to the Château Hôtel des Écuries where we would plot our next moves. Uncle Sam had to make "a quick phone call" so we waited for him in one of the hotel's meeting rooms where we had a view of the inn's horse stables out the window. Storm loves horses.

"Excuse me," she said to the server who brought us a tray of coffee and pastries. "Does that beautiful white horse in the stables have a name?"

"*Oui*," said the man in a natty hotel uniform

as he poured out tiny cups of espresso coffee for everybody, even those of us who hate espresso and coffee. "That is Crème de la Crème. She is the best of the best."

"*Merci*," said Storm.

While Storm gawked out the window at the horsey with the flowing blond mane, the rest of us gobbled down madeleines, éclairs, macarons, petit fours, and opera cake (which was way better than opera all by itself). It was all very delicious and extremely sugary.

"Sorry to keep you waiting," said Uncle Sam when he stepped into the meeting room. "Urgent business at the State Department."

"They won't hurt my mother and father, will they?" asked Fiona, sounding terrified.

"No, ma'am," said Uncle Sam. "The State Department doesn't hurt people. That's our job."

Fiona blubbered a little when he said that.

"Don't worry," Tommy assured her. "Nobody is going to hurt your mother and father."

"Unless they hurt our mother and father," said Beck.

"Totally," said Tommy. "They do that, all bets are off."

Fiona blubbered some more. I slid her the pastries. There wasn't much left on the platter except a couple of fruit tarts. She waved the tray away.

"So, tell me what you learned in the dungeon," said Uncle Sam.

"That we need to be in Israel," I reported.

"How come?" asked Tommy.

"Because that's where our mom and dad are most likely being taken by her mom and dad." I did a head bob toward Fiona.

"The historic walled port city of Acre in northwest Israel," said Storm. "Also known to the locals as Akko."

Uncle Sam nodded slowly. He was catching on. "The last stronghold of the Knights Templar."

"Correct," said Storm. "Its capture in 1291 by the Mamluk sultan Al-Ashraf Khalil marked the end of the Crusaders' rule in the Holy Land. It was the last stand of the Knights Templar."

We then showed Uncle Sam the photos we'd taken on our phones of the graffiti scratched into the dungeon walls and the stack of symbols (treasure, bear, Jerusalem cross, castle) pointing us to that particular spot in Israel.

"Brilliant!" said Uncle Sam, slapping both his hands on the conference table and standing up. "I'll arrange transportation. We'll depart for Israel first thing tomorrow morning! Hopefully, we can find the Knights Templar treasure before your parents find it for those greedy, grasping, money-grubbing Glendennings!" He turned to Fiona. "No offense intended."

"None taken," said Fiona, fighting back tears.

"Get some rest, Kidds. When we arrive in Israel, you four need to do your best to outthink, outwit, and outplay your parents!"

"Huh?" said Tommy.

"If we can find the treasure before they do, we'll be in a position to nab their captors and facilitate your parents' rescue!"

"I want to be there, too," said Fiona.

"Yes," said Uncle Sam, nodding thoughtfully. "You might prove to be a very valuable bargaining chip should your parents become...difficult."

CHAPTER 34

Okay, that last little threat totally freaked out Fiona.

"They won't become difficult!" she told Uncle Sam. "I promise! I can get through to them. I know I can!"

"Then pack your bag, Ms. Glendenning. We leave at oh-six-hundred hours."

We all headed upstairs to the room Tommy and I were sharing. Fiona went to her own room. She needed some "alone time" to pack her bag and process all the new information about her mom and dad. I couldn't blame her. I would've needed some major alone time, too, if my parents had abandoned me so they could run off and create a phony cult whose only real purpose was to go hunting for medieval treasure.

At least our parents took us with them on treasure hunts. And, as far as we knew, they hadn't invented any crazed cults based on beliefs they didn't really believe. It was pretty clear from what Knight Rodrigo had told us that Mr. and Mrs. Glendenning (and their army of knights and ladies) were only in this whole modern-day Templar thing for the money. And the gold. And the jewels. They probably wanted the jewels, too.

While Tommy, Storm, and I paced around the room, trying to think up some way to do the impossible (be smarter, sharper, and faster than Mom and Dad), Beck dug out a pair of AR dive goggles from a duffel bag and slipped them on. Yes, it reminded me of when she constantly wore those 3D glasses before Mom was kidnapped the first time.

"I'm drawing a blank," said Beck, stumbling around with her arms extended.

"Because the computer's not on," I reminded her.

"Of course!" said Storm, slapping a palm to her forehead. "The laptop!"

"Don't worry," said Tommy. "I didn't lose it. It's been in my backpack and on my back all day long."

"Let me see it!" said Storm.

"Oh, you don't trust me?" said Tommy, slipping out of the backpack's harness straps. "You think I lost the laptop somehow?"

"No, Tommy. I think the laptop might confirm that we're heading in the right direction."

"Oh. Okay. Confirmation is cool."

Storm unzippered the cargo compartment and

pulled the computer out of its protective foam pocket.

"What are we looking for?" I asked.

"Augmented reality data," said Storm, booting up the computer. "The goggles Beck's wearing only work when they're fed information from this hard drive." She tapped some keys and opened up the ginormous data file. "Here we go. Just as I thought. There is historical, architectural, and geographic information for several locations. Thonis-Heracleion, of course, off the coast of Egypt."

"Been there," said Tommy. "Dived that. Saw Cleopatra."

"That was just a test run," said Storm.

"For what?" I asked.

"All these other locations." She pointed to the index with its list of files. "Places where various sources have claimed that the Knights Templar buried their treasure. Oak Island, Nova Scotia. Rosslyn Chapel, Scotland. Temple Bruer, Lincolnshire, England. Bornholm Island, Denmark. Trinity Church, New York City. Château de Gisors, where we were earlier."

"So we could've used the AR goggles to see what the place used to look like in the olden days?" asked Tommy.

"Yep."

"That would've been so cool."

"Let's go back and do it!" I suggested.

"Bick?" said Storm. "We're in a hurry, remember? We're going to Israel, and guess what?"

"What?"

"We're on the right track. The last data file Dad and Mom loaded onto the hard drive?"

"Yeah?"

"It's for Acre in Israel!"

CHAPTER 35

That night, I couldn't sleep.

Not just because I was excited about flying off to the Holy Land, where we'd retrace the steps of the Crusaders.

No, I couldn't sleep because Storm had double-triple-dared me to eat escargot for dinner even though they are escar-gross. Chewy, slimy snails cooked in garlic butter.

But I gulped one down.

I know, I know. I should've just stuck to my usual dinner—a crusty hunk of bread. Now, hours after gulping down a SLIMY SNAIL, my stomach was gurgling. Worse, I imagined that the burbling in my belly was the sound of the angry snail I'd swallowed slithering and sliding around inside my intestines looking for its long-lost shell!

That's how come I was wide awake when our hotel room door creaked open at two a.m.

And why I saw a shadowy figure tiptoeing across our room.

The silhouette was vaguely familiar. A long-legged man in a beret with a pipe jutting out of his mouth. He snuck over to the chair where Tommy had hung his backpack. The man wiggled his long, gloved fingers to limber them up. Then carefully, very carefully, he plucked the bag off the back of the chair.

I flicked on a bedside table lamp.

The man froze.

Now I completely recognized the guy. It was the local we met the other night. In the restaurant. When Tommy was flirting with Fiona, showing her our AR goggles. The French man was still wearing a white turtleneck under a corduroy blazer.

"*Excusez-moi,*" he said, with a very polite tip of

his beret. *"Au revoir et bonne nuit."*

He took off running across the room like a startled stork. He cradled the backpack in both arms and bolted out the door.

"Thief!" I shouted. "Backpack thief!"

Tommy popped up in bed. "What the...?"

Storm and Beck hurtled into our room.

"That man running down the staircase has our backpack!" said Beck.

"Shhh!" said Storm. "Quiet. We don't want to alarm Uncle Sam or the CIA agents."

"Why not?" I whispered back. "They have weapons. They can stop the guy!"

"And," said Storm, "when they do, they'll find out about the valuable data stored on our laptop's hard drive. Right now, Uncle Sam doesn't even know we have the laptop!"

"So?" said Beck.

"So," said Tommy, "do either of you guys trust anybody named Uncle or Aunt with that kind of info? Other than Uncle Richie, of course."

"Of course," said Storm.

Beck and I looked at each other. We remembered

evil and weird Uncle Timothy as well as sometimes devious and double-crossing Aunt Bela Kilgore. It would probably be best if we kept a few secrets from Uncle Sam.

Outside, I heard the unmistakable clatter of a bike chain and the tinkle of a bike bell. I raced to the window. The gangly man in the beret was riding away with our backpack stuffed inside the white wicker basket attached to his front handlebars.

"That's him!" I said. "He's getting away. He's on a bicycle!"

"Of course he is," said Beck. "He's French!"

Storm grinned. "Don't worry. He won't get far. You three grab bikes off the front porch and follow me."

"Huh?" I said.

"What're you gonna ride?" asked Tommy.

"The best of the best," said Storm, sounding super excited.

Yep. You guessed it.

Storm charged out of the hotel and into the stables where she climbed aboard that beautiful

THERE'S A REASON THIS HORSE'S HOOVES THUNDER. STORM RIDES AGAIN!

white horse with the flowing blond mane. Riding bareback, she tore off down the road.

The poor French guy puffing his pipe on the bike wouldn't stand a chance.

Storm and her trusty steed were gunning for him.

CHAPTER 36

Storm galloped away on her trusty steed.

The horse's pounding hooves made the earth tremble. The rest of us hurried over to where the hotel had a rack of bicycles for guests to borrow. We each grabbed one and pedaled after Storm, knowing we'd never catch up with her.

Storm's a champion rider.

Whenever we were on dry land during our early years of treasure hunting, she'd take riding lessons or enter equestrian competitions. Her room on board *The Lost* had all sorts of blue ribbons hanging on the walls. I guess those ribbons were soggy now, at the bottom of the Mediterranean

Sea, thanks to Fiona Glendenning's scheming mom and dad!

"That poor French guy doesn't stand a chance," said Beck as we pedaled down the dark road after Storm.

"Chya," said Tommy. "Did you see the clouds in Storm's eyes?"

In case you didn't know, Storm's real name is Stephanie. But nobody calls her that. Except Mom, Dad, and Uncle Richie. She got her nickname because, even though it doesn't happen very often, when she gets angry, her eyes become a pair of dark thunderhead clouds bubbling up and blacking out the sky on a steamy tropical day. Then she explodes in lightning and fury.

We followed the sound of the horse hooves and the occasional "HIYA!" from Storm. There were also assorted whinnies and nickers. The horse Storm was riding seemed to be enjoying the chase as much as she was.

Our big sister is also a pretty good roper. Some of the ribbons on her cabin wall came from rodeo competitions. So by the time we caught up with

YOUR SISTER WAS NOT HORSING AROUND WHEN SHE CHASED AFTER ME.
IT WAS A SPUR-OF-THE-MOMENT DECISION.

her, Storm had the French guy all tied up and lashed to a fence post.

She was also holding Tommy's backpack.

"*Sacre bleu!*" the man sputtered super smoothly, the way only a suave French criminal could. "*Je suis vraiment désolé. Je dois présenter des excuses.*"

"Huh?" said Tommy.

"He says he is so sorry and must apologize," Storm translated.

"*Oui!*"

I took over the translation. "Now he said, 'Yes.'"

"Duh," said Beck. "We all know that one."

"*Oui, oui,*" said Tommy. Then he giggled. "I said wee-wee."

"You guys?" said Storm. Her eyes looked like they were about to shift into Tropical Storm Warning mode again.

"Sorry," said Tommy. "Okay, pal." He turned to the French guy. "Spill. Why'd you steal my backpack?"

"PA!" the man said, spitting out his pipe, which

he kind of had to do because his hands were tied behind his back. "Why should I tell you children anything?"

"Because you're our prisoner!" I said.

"So? I am working for a very high-level American spy! He wanted to know what was inside this, how you say, pack of the back!"

Uncle Sam! I realized. He was the "high-level American spy." He didn't know what we had stashed in our backpack but, apparently, he would pay good money to find out!

"How much is this spy paying you?" asked Storm.

"*Beaucoup.* A lot."

"More than this?" Storm held out a gold coin that glittered in the moonlight.

"Wait a second," I said. "Is that the gold coin we found hidden in the sub crypt of the Rosslyn Chapel? The one that led us to Château de Gisors?"

"*Oui*," said Storm with a shrug. "It was just lying there on the floor. After our so-called tour guide, Fiona, handed it to me, I slipped it into my pocket. Guess what? I did a little research. Turns out this is a very rare antique. Worth maybe several thousand dollars."

The French man licked his lips and made a quick decision.

"The very high-level American spy is only paying me one hundred euros," he blurted. "He is a high-ranking government official for the United States, which, I think, is why his code name is Uncle Sam. However, he is not very imaginative. His code name for me is Frère Jacques."

The instant he said it, Beck and I started humming. We were about to launch into a rousing round on the "*dormez vous*" bit when Tommy and Storm shot us a look. We took the hint. There were no more *ding dong ding*s.

"The spy has to be Uncle Sam," I whispered.

"Well, duh," said Beck.

"That was *très* obvious, Bick," added Tommy.

"I was to bring the purloined knapsack to this American secret agent man before he departs from France for parts unknown very early this morning. Our rendezvous is scheduled for five o'clock in the a.m. *Mon Dieu!* That is only two hours from now."

Storm looked inside the backpack and nodded. That meant the laptop was still safe and snug inside. "Can you miss that meeting with the spy?" She rolled the gold coin around between her fingers. "Can you forget you ever met this Uncle Sam or ever snagged this backpack?"

"*Oui.* For the right price, I can forget many things. I could also disappear and take a vacation to the South of France. A long vacation. I know a very disreputable jeweler in Marseille who is always looking to buy rare gold coins from those who know how to keep their mouths shut."

"Perfect. Untie him, Tommy."

Tommy did. The French man rubbed at his wrists. Storm tossed him the gold coin.

"*Merci*, children. I will now disappear into the night! Let us forget we ever met. *Au revoir!*"

He hopped on board his bike and wobbled away.

"Uncle Sam," said Tommy, punching his fist into his open palm the same way he did whenever anybody mentioned the name Nathan Collier.

"He's up to something," I said.

"Yeah," said Beck. "Something no good."

Storm slipped the laptop out of its protective foam slot and hurled Tommy's black backpack up and over the fence. Storm has a good arm. The thing flew across the grassy field and landed with a wet smack in what sounded like a mud puddle.

"Hey!" said Tommy. "I had hair gel in the front flap of that bag!"

"Sorry. But we have to make Uncle Sam think that his asset, Frère Jacques, stole the backpack but double-crossed him by not turning it over."

"Okay. I guess. I had suntan lotion in there, too."

"We'll buy you a fresh tube. Come on." She went over to where her horse was grazing on the grass.

"Where are we going?" I asked.

"On my ride through town," said Storm, "I passed a twenty-four-hour drug store. They'll have suntan lotion and Ace bandages."

"Why do we need Ace bandages?" asked Beck.

"So I can strap this laptop to my back and hide it underneath that blousy cotton kaftan I picked up at the souk in Egypt."

"Excellent idea, Storm!" said Tommy.

She nodded. "Yes. Plus, a laptop strapped to the small of my back might make me stand up straighter. It'll be good for my posture."

CHAPTER 37

As scheduled, Beck, Storm, and I met Uncle Sam in the lobby of the hotel at six a.m. (one hour after he was supposed to meet with the thieving Frère Jacques).

Storm of course was wearing her bright-blue and blousy kaftan. She was also standing up very straight.

Tommy wasn't with us yet. He would soon be making the dramatic entrance I'd scripted for him.

Fiona was already in the lobby, nibbling at her nails and looking like a nervous gerbil. I guess realizing that your parents dumped you so they could run off and become criminal masterminds by pretending to be medieval knights will do that to you.

Six CIA agents, decked out in navy-blue windbreakers, flanked Uncle Sam. All of them were wearing sunglasses even though, like I said, it was six o'clock in the morning and we were inside!

Finally, Tommy came stomping down the staircase from the second floor.

"I've been robbed! Robbed, I tell you!"

"What?" said Uncle Sam, as if he didn't know what had transpired up in our room a few hours earlier.

"Somebody stole my backpack!" Tommy continued, having memorized what I told him to say. "I can't find it anywhere. And, oh, how I have looked. High and low. Low and high. Someone must've snuck into our room while we were all sleeping and stolen it! I think it was a French guy because whoever it was left quite a trail of flaky baguette bread crumbs on the floor."

“Are you sure it’s missing, Tommy?” said Beck, reciting her line perfectly.

“Yes! It’s gone! Gone, I tell you.”

And...*scene*. That was the end of our script.

“Is there any coffee or croissants?” Tommy asked, completely breaking character. “I’m starving.”

“Thomas?” said Uncle Sam. “If I may—what was in that backpack?”

“Valuable stuff.”

Uncle Sam took off his shades. He was extremely interested. “Such as?”

“Socks. The wicking kind. They eliminate odors and keep your feet dry. I also had hair gel in the front flap.”

“So, nothing in your backpack would help us in our quest to find the Knights Templar treasure?”

“Well, dry feet are always a plus on any treasure hunt.”

Uncle Sam closed his eyes in total frustration. “Mount up, people. We need to be Oscar Mike!”

"On the move!" we all responded like we were the Kidd family choir.

We'd fooled Uncle Sam. Just like Storm said, he thought Frère Jacques had double-crossed him and kept Tommy's backpack and all its contents for himself. He also probably thought there was nothing valuable inside the bag. Unless you were really into high-tech hiking socks.

CHAPTER 38

We boarded another jet.

This one was more like a commercial airliner with rows and rows of seating.

When we walked up the center aisle, we noticed some very interesting dignitaries up front in the first-class cabin. They appeared to be Saudi sheiks. There were four of them, all men. All wearing thawbs—the white, long-sleeved, ankle-length garments that were even blousier than Storm's kaftan. They also had the traditional square cotton scarves on their heads, what Storm called a keffiyeh or shemagh.

"What's with the oil sheiks?" Tommy whispered.

"Shhh!" said Storm. "We don't know what business these men are in."

True, I thought. They could be diplomats.

Or international spies.

Because Uncle Sam took a seat in the first-class cabin with them.

Once we were airborne and the seat belt sign was turned off, Uncle Sam ordered the flight

attendants to pull the cabin-separating curtain across the aisle to block our view of whatever might be going on up front.

I did, however, hear Uncle Sam say, "We have much to discuss, gentlemen," right before the curtain closed.

One of us needed to eavesdrop on that conversation. And since Beck always draws me with jug-handle ears, I figured it better be me.

I tapped Storm.

"Cover me," I whispered.

She nodded. Then she stood up.

"Ladies and gentlemen?" she said, addressing the CIA agents seated in the coach section of the plane with us. "Since we're on our way to Acre, Israel, I thought it might be beneficial if I gave you all some background information on our destination."

The spies all rolled their eyes and opened their paperback novels or tapped the TV screens in the seatbacks in front of their faces. They were all actively avoiding eye contact with Storm, who gave her most boring Wikipedia data dump ever.

"Acre sits in a natural harbor in the Haifa Bay on the coast of the Mediterranean's Levantine Sea."

And blah, blah, blah.

When she launched into the super boring bit about Acre during the early Bronze Age, nobody was looking our way. Some of the CIA team were snoozing. I dropped to the floor and crawled underneath the seats in front of us. I'm pretty wiry and sinewy so I slithered along easily. (Okay, Beck says I'm just skinny. With arms like toothpicks. She says my butt reminds her of Flat Stanley's.)

I was able to wiggle my way to the front of the cabin. Just off to the side of the curtain, I could hear everything Uncle Sam and his guests had to say.

"Those children in the back belong to Thomas and Sue Kidd," said Uncle Sam.

"The famous treasure hunters?" asked one of the Saudi sheikhs.

"That's right. They're the ones who were kidnapped by your competition. If a treasure can be found, the Kidds will be the ones to find it."

"And so you are following these kidnappers?"

"Precisely. We'll continue to shadow them and will steal the treasure from our adversaries immediately after Dr. and Mrs. Kidd locate it. I had hoped that the Kidd children might have certain information we could use to assist us in our own quest for the Templar treasure. But it turns out all the children had were socks."

"Excuse me?"

"It's not important. What is important is that, one way or another, you gentlemen will soon have your treasure returned to you."

"Yes," said another Saudi sheikh with a deep and rumbling voice. "For it is not, as you mistakenly labeled it, the Knights Templar treasure. It is ours. It was stolen from our ancestors during the Crusades."

"Well," said Uncle Sam, "not to be difficult, but some of the gold did come from Europeans."

"It is all ours! Reparations for what your Crusaders did to our holy land many centuries ago!"

"I agree, Your Excellency..."

“Good, Mr. Heenehan. You should. For if you and your comrades at the State Department sincerely wish to build your new air force base on our sovereign territory, you will not only find our treasure, you will gladly turn it over to us. All of it!”

“That’s the plan, Your Excellency.”

“Marvelous. Then we are in agreement.”

“Roger that. Returning the treasure to you, its rightful owners, is and always has been the number one priority of this operation.”

Really?

I thought finding our parents and rescuing them from their kidnappers was priority number one. At least that’s what Uncle Sam had told us.

The guy could never have been a member of the Knights Templar.

He lied too much.

But now I knew the truth.

When it came to rescuing Mom and Dad, we Kidds were, once again, on our own.

CHAPTER 39

"All right, everybody, take the rest of the day off," said Uncle Sam when we arrived at our hotel in Acre, Israel.

Seriously? I thought. *Take the day off?*

It was only three o'clock in the afternoon.

How'd this guy ever become a top spy? Did secret agents only work half days?

"You Kidds can explore the city," he continued. "Here's some Israeli money." He handed Tommy a wad of paper money and a handful of clinking coins. "The currency here is shekels."

"Actually," said Storm, "the plural of shekel is 'shekalim.' The shekel is divided into one hundred agora..."

“Oh-kay,” said Uncle Sam, cutting off Storm before she could give us the going exchange rate of a shekel to a dollar. (Somewhere around thirty cents, she told us later.) “Why don’t you kids go on a tour of the city? I’m sure Storm can point out all sorts of, uh, interesting sites. Team? Upstairs. Bring the equipment.” Uncle Sam and the rest of his CIA crew hustled across the lobby of the Efendi Hotel toting their bags and metal cargo cases. Fiona followed after them.

“I’m going upstairs to take a nap,” she said with a big hand-to-mouth yawn as a bellhop came over and picked up her rolling suitcase.

The hotel was set inside two Ottoman palaces made out of stone that overlooked the Mediterranean Sea. The lobby was extremely swanky-looking.

I was thinking about how those four very wealthy-looking travelers in the first-class cabin of our jetliner from France probably would’ve loved the Efendi Hotel. But they were no longer with us. Before landing in Israel, we’d touched down in Saudi Arabia to drop them off.

"Grab your gear, you guys," Tommy whispered, picking up his duffel. "Before one of those bellhops comes over here and hauls our bags up to our rooms."

"Good idea," said Beck, grabbing her bag.

Yep, we'd carried our wet suits, snorkels, and the three augmented reality dive masks (not to mention the laptop, which was, of course, the brains of the whole AR system) all the way from Egypt to Scotland to France to Israel.

OUR BAGS ARE WORLD TRAVELLERS, TOO.

I had a hunch we'd be needing the gear soon. Very soon.

We'd probably need to rent a couple of scuba tanks, too. We hadn't been lugging *those* halfway around the world and back again.

"We're close, you guys," I said. "The Templar treasure is somewhere here in Acre! I can smell it."

"No," said Beck. "That's just you again, Bick."

"Didn't we have a deodorant discussion earlier, bro?" asked Tommy.

"We can talk about that later," said Storm. "Come on. We need to find a place where we can plot our next moves."

"Yeah," I said. "Uncle Sam might be taking the rest of the day off, but not us! True treasure hunters never rest!"

CHAPTER 40

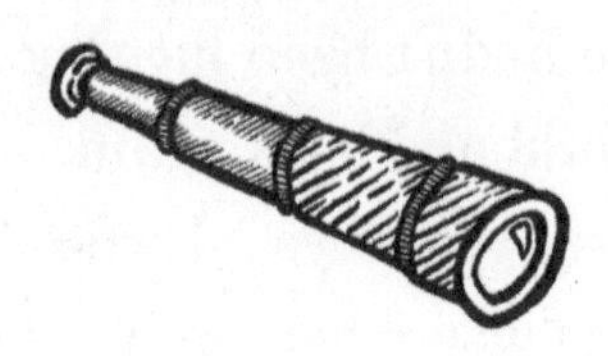

Coffee Rzaz, a cafe that served sandwiches on great-tasting bread, was right on the water with an excellent palm-tree-framed view of the deep-blue Mediterranean Sea.

(Okay, Beck says they also served salads. But who needs salad when there's warm pita bread and hummus?)

The cafe also had outdoor seating and excellent Wi-Fi, so we placed our orders and set up shop.

"Here, Storm," said Tommy awkwardly. "Why don't you try on this dive mask while I google what this squishy slimy stuff is on top of my salad?"

Tommy was talking very loudly so anybody

SLURP!
TAP TAP
WHAT WE SAW IN REAL REALITY
WHAT STORM SAW IN AUGMENTED REALITY

who thought it was weird to see an American girl wearing a dive mask at an outdoor Israeli cafe table would have a reasonable explanation for why Storm looked so ridiculous. Tommy was also concocting a plausible reason for him to be tapping away on a laptop keyboard, even though people always do that at cafes. In truth, Tommy and Storm were activating one pair of the augmented reality dive masks. Storm slipped it on. Tommy hit Return. Miniature green LEDs glowed along the mask's rubbery edges.

"Bring up what you have on Acre," Storm whispered.

"On it," said Tommy, clacking the keyboard.

"What do you see?" Beck whispered eagerly.

"What used to be right here!" said Storm with a gasp. "Back during the days of the Knights Templar. We're talking 1290 CE! I can see the outlines of a stone curtain wall like you'd see between towers on a medieval castle!"

Storm slowly turned her head to the right. Then she slowly turned it to the left. I knew what she was up to: scanning the whole area and memorizing everything that Mom and Dad's architectural data was telling her. She was making a mental map for us.

"Bigger fortress to the south," she mumbled. "In the same spot as that small cove where all those waves are crashing against the rocks. That site is labeled as the former location of the Knights Templar fortress and treasure tower."

"Treasure tower?" I gasped. Out loud. Fortunately, even out loud, my gasps aren't very loud. But I still earned a dirty look from Beck and Tommy. Even Storm whirled around to glare at me. (I wondered what the augmented reality mask showed overlapping my head. Probably a lot of empty space because it was pretty dumb for me to blurt out the T-word like that in public.)

Storm sighed and swung her head and dive mask to the north.

"Nothing of any significance to the north," she reported. "Just more wall connecting with the wall that's actually there."

Acre still had a lot of its medieval stacked-stone seawall intact.

Storm stood up, walked across the parking lot with both her arms extended, and kind of stumbled blindly toward a street.

"That's good, sis," said Tommy for the benefit of anybody watching Storm doing her Frankenstein-ish march across the parking lot. "Take a little walk. Make sure your dive mask stays snug and secure. You don't want it coming loose when, you know, you're moving around underwater."

"Yeah," I said, trying to help Tommy sell the scene. "Always best to do your dive gear fittings on dry land."

Storm reached the street, pivoted to the east, and paused.

Something she saw up that narrow lane seemed to excite her, because she whipped off the dive mask and hurried back to our table.

"There's a Templar tunnel entrance!" she said. "About five blocks up that street. The tunnel burrows under the city and, according to Mom and

Dad's data, leads to an underground guardhouse."

"What's after the guardhouse?" I asked as quietly as I could.

"Another tunnel. One that, eventually, leads to the T.T."

I nodded.

Because I knew what T.T. was code for: treasure tower!

CHAPTER 41

Beck passed Storm her sketchbook.

"Here," she said. "Draw the map."

Storm shook her head. "No need." She tapped her temple. "It's all up here."

"Yeah," I said, "but we'd kind of like to see it."

"We love treasure maps," said Beck.

I nodded. "Especially all the dashes and the clever landmarks—like palm trees or boulders—and then the big *X* marking the spot."

"Sorry, you two," said Storm. "We don't want this information falling into the wrong hands. So let's just keep it stored and photographically memorized in my head. Besides, there aren't any palm trees inside a tunnel."

Tommy closed the laptop and stowed it inside his nylon duffel. "Storm's right. We keep the treasure tower a secret." He zipped his bag and nudged it under the table, out of sight.

A server brought over a bill for our food and drinks. Tommy looked at it. For nearly a minute. Then he gave up and passed the green slip of paper and all the Israeli money Uncle Sam had given him over to Storm.

"Um, can you figure out these shekels?" he asked.

"The plural of shekel is 'shekalim,'" Storm reminded him.

"Riiiiight."

"So," I said, rubbing my hands together eagerly, "when do we set off for the treasure tower?"

"What treasure tower?"

Uncle Sam stepped out of the shadow cast by the umbrella at the table next to ours. Fiona was with him.

Beck, Storm, and Tommy turned to me. We needed a cover story. Fast. And since I'm the family tale teller, I went to work.

"The fabled Terrifying Treasure Tower of Kathmandu. It's on our list of where we're going to explore next, once we find Mom and Dad. So, duh, I guess I just answered my own question. We head to the Treasure Tower of Kathmandu after you guys rescue Mom and Dad. Of course, the tower isn't in Kathmandu. That's why it's so darn hard to find. It's actually high up in the Himalayan mountains ringing the Kathmandu Valley. This tower is like a giant Jenga tower, only, instead of wooden blocks, it's a stack of solid gold slabs the size of tractor trailers. The trick is, first, you need a cargo container crane. Those are hard to haul up mountains. Then, you have to remove the ginormous gold bars, one at a time, without making the tower topple. If you knock it over, the locals typically laugh at you and then boil you in oil like you're an onion ring or a deep-fried Twinkie."

Uncle Sam was giving me a look. Like I was an idiot. It's the same look Beck gives me some of the time. (Okay, a lot of the time.)

Then he pointed at the dive mask sitting next to Storm's hummus bowl.

"What's that?" he asked.

"A dive mask," said Storm.

Uncle Sam narrowed his eyes into tiny slits. "Is it, somehow, designed to help you locate the Templar treasure?"

Storm hesitated. So, once again, I jumped in.

"You betcha. For instance, let's say the Templar treasure is underwater, somewhere out there in the Mediterranean Sea. The dive mask will help keep the salt water out of our eyes, which can sting because, hello, it's extremely salty water. If you don't have a dive mask, you just have to close your eyes, feel your way, and hope you bump into—"

"Enough!" Uncle Sam barked as he snatched up the dive mask from the table.

"Hey," said Storm, "that's ours."

"Not anymore. I'm confiscating it. And why aren't you children searching for your parents?"

"Um, you told us to take the day off," Tommy reminded the lazy spy.

"That was just a clever ruse!" Uncle Sam snatched a shekel off the table. He sounded angry.

Frustrated. "We were hoping you four would strike off on your own, follow some secret clue, and find the treasure. That's why we've been tracking you. But, noooooo. You children aren't the treasure hunters you're reputed to be! You're nothing but deadweight! And, quite frankly, I'm tired of wasting precious time and governmental assets hoping you'll, somehow, point me in the right direction!"

Oh, yeah.

Uncle Sam was angry. So angry, he totally blew his own cover and, for maybe the first time, told us the truth.

CHAPTER 42

Uncle Sam held up one of the shekel coins.

Guess it was actually a high-tech tracking device worth a lot more than thirty cents. Good thing we hadn't used it to buy a Coke from a vending machine.

Uncle Sam shook his head. He was soooooo disappointed in us.

"You Kidd kids are so worthless. You four came to this coffee shop, ordered a meal, and you haven't budged since."

"The bread's delish," I said in our defense. "Warm and puffy."

"You're supposed to be some of the boldest, most courageous, most intrepid young treasure hunters in the world? Ha! You have just been wasting my time."

"Are you forgetting all that cool stuff we figured out in Scotland and France?" said Tommy, defensively.

"Yesterday's news. What have you done for me today?"

"What you told us to do," said Beck. "WE TOOK THE AFTERNOON OFF!"

"Well, take the rest of the week off," said Uncle Sam. "Take the whole month."

He reached into his suit coat and pulled out five airplane ticket vouchers and another bundle of cash.

"Find your own hotel rooms. Organize your own meals. And take the first flight home to wherever home might be. We no longer require or want your assistance."

"Um, that's five airplane ticket vouchers," I said. "There are only four of us."

He did a head nod toward Fiona. "We don't

require Miss Glendenning's assistance any longer, either."

"What about our parents?" asked Beck.

Uncle Sam shrugged like he couldn't care less. "We'll try to find them. But locating the Templar treasure has always been and will always remain our top priority."

"But you said—"

"Yeah. I was lying. Spies do that. Get used to it, kid. Never trust anything we say. Have a safe flight and enjoy the rest of your lives."

Uncle Sam stomped away to where a sleek black sedan had just squealed to a stop at the curb.

He climbed into the car. It screeched away.

"Whoa," I said. "What a rude dude."

Beck agreed. "Totally."

"Guess we're on our own now," said Fiona.

"Yeah," said Tommy sadly. He didn't even wiggle or waggle his eyebrows at Fiona. "I guess we are."

CHAPTER 43

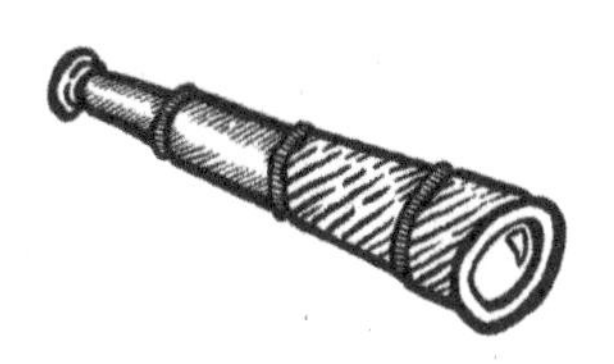

"We should work together," said Fiona. She found an empty chair and scootched it over to our table.

Beck raised a skeptical eyebrow. "Work together? On what?"

"Finding our parents," said Fiona. "Come on—you guys aren't really going to give up your search and go home, are you?"

None of us said a word. And not just because, thanks to Fiona's mom, we really didn't have a home anymore. Our ship burned and sank off the coast of Egypt thanks to Mrs. Glendenning and her gang of wacky pirates.

Finally, Tommy slid one of the airline vouchers across the table. "Take it, Fiona. Fly home to Scotland. I think you and I need to become better strangers."

"What?"

"Hello? Are you in a tunnel? Because we're breaking up."

"We were never together, Tommy."

"Sure. Tell yourself whatever you need to hear to ease the pain."

"Look, Thomas," said Fiona, "I want to find your parents, too!"

"Oh, really?" I said as sarcastically as I could.

"Why on earth would you want to do that?" added Beck. She was downright snarky.

"Because," said Fiona, "*my* mother and father will be with *your* mother and father."

"Chya," said Tommy. "But your folks will be the kidnappers. Our parents will be the kidnappees. So..."

"They're still my mom and dad!" Fiona protested. "They've just fallen in with the wrong crowd. They've been brainwashed. The whole

Knights Templar thing is some kind of cult."

"Um, but aren't they the leaders?" I asked.

"Yes. For now. Because they don't realize that what they're doing is wrong. Why do you think I became a Knights Templar scholar? So I could, one day, become a history professor and lecture them about how foolishly they're behaving."

"Um, does that day have to be today?" asked Beck.

"Think of me as an insurance policy."

"As in dull and boring?" said Storm.

"No! I mean if you find your parents and they're being held hostage by my parents, I'll have a better chance of talking my mom and dad out of doing something stupid or violent than you guys would on your own."

We all thought about that for a few seconds.

Finally, Storm reluctantly nodded. "Fiona makes a valid point. You guys? I think we should take her up on her offer. She might prove useful in our upcoming quest."

"Fine," I said.

"Whatever," said Beck.

Then we both sighed very dramatically and simultaneously rolled our eyes. It's a twin thing.

"Cool," said Tommy, with a flirty wink to Fiona. "So, I guess this is a date, huh?"

"No, Tommy," said Storm. "This is a rescue mission!"

"What about the treasure hunt?" asked Fiona.

Beck, Tommy, and I shot a sideways glance at Storm. She gave us a slight, barely perceptible, teensy little head shake.

No. We were not sharing our augmented reality information and discoveries with Fiona Glendenning. We were not telling her about the tunnel burrowing under Acre on its way to the Knights Templar treasure tower.

"Mom and Dad are the greatest treasures on earth," I said, to cover the awkward pause.

"I realize that," said Fiona, sounding slightly exasperated with us. "But if the five of us can find the Templar treasure before your parents are forced to find it for my parents, we'll have all the ransom we needed to secure their release!"

Suddenly, I heard a weird ringtone. It was

that "Auld Lang Syne" tune that people sing at midnight on New Year's Eve. You know: "Should old acquaintance be forgot, and never brought to mind"? It's a Scottish song.

"I don't believe this," said Fiona, studying the face of her phone.

"What?" said Tommy.

"That's their ringtone."

"Who?"

"My mom and dad!"

CHAPTER 44

"Mom?" Fiona said to the caller. "Why, it's been years since we've spoken. Where are you?"

Fiona listened, then covered her phone with her hand. "She's here. In Acre! Dad's here, too."

I rolled my hand repeatedly to indicate that we were much more interested in other, more important information.

"You have Dr. and Mrs. Kidd?" said Fiona. Then she shot us a big thumbs-up with her free hand. We all leaned in, straining to hear the other side of the phone conversation.

"They art fine, Fiona," I heard her mom say in

a phony English accent. "Howsoever, they haveth not been most keen on aiding us in our noble quest for our rightful treasure. Art thou with their children as our spies doth profess?"

"Mom?"

"Yes, Fiona?"

"Drop the accent. You don't do it very well."

There was a pause. "Still as defiant and difficult as ever, eh, Fiona?"

"I am my mother's daughter."

"Very well. We need to meet."

"Where?"

"The Khan al-Umdan in the Old City. The Inn of the Columns."

"Is that, like, a hotel?" asked Tommy.

"Who was that?" snapped Fiona's mom.

"Thomas Kidd," said Fiona, her voice steely and strong. "Dr. and Mrs. Kidd's oldest son."

Tommy leaned in closer to the phone. "Fiona and I were kind of dating. But, hello? This whole kidnapping thing totally destroyed the mood. Major buzzkill, Mrs. G."

“Are the other Kidd children with you as well?” asked Mrs. Glendenning.

“Yes, Mother. They are all very eager to rescue their mother and father.”

“Good. For we hath a proposition to maketh.”

“Mom? You’re doing it again! These aren’t the Middle Ages. Knock it off!”

“Fine. Meet me at Khan al-Umdan. In ten minutes. It’s not far from where you are now.”

“How do you know—”

“Ten minutes, Fiona. Bring the Kidds. We have much to discuss.”

“Will Father be there?”

“No. He will be guarding our hostages. And if those clever Kidd children try anything funny…”

“Don’t worry,” I said. “We lost all our whoopee cushions and hand buzzers when our ship sank!”

“Yeah!” shouted Beck. “Remember that little unfortunate incident at sea? By the way, how many helicopters do you people own?”

We heard a bloop noise. The call went dead.

“She hung up,” muttered Fiona.

“The Khan al-Umdan isn’t very far,” said

Storm, accessing her internal Google Maps capabilities. "We'll be there in plenty of time if we leave now." She plunked some of our Israeli money down on the table and led the way out of the cafe. She was also eyeballing Fiona suspiciously.

But, of course, as soon as we were all up and walking, Storm continued her Wikipedia data dump on the Inn of the Columns.

"It was built in 1784 on the site of the Royal Customs House of the Kingdom of Jerusalem. Its forty columns are made of granite, some salvaged from the ruins of the Crusaders' final fortress..."

"Um, Storm?" said Tommy. "Can we focus on something that we should know before we have this meeting with Fiona's evil mother?"

"She's not evil," Fiona protested.

"Matter of opinion," I mumbled out of the corner of my mouth.

"Fine," said Storm. "It's a major tourist attraction. There'll probably be a crowd. I don't think Mrs. Glendenning will try anything sneaky."

"Even though she's evil." This time, it was

Beck mumbling out of the corner of her mouth.

We soon reached the Khan al-Umdan. It looked like an open-air market fenced in on an all four sides by a two-story stone building filled with arches. There was a tall clock tower rising over the main entrance.

"This used to be a warehouse," Storm explained, because, apparently, she'd only hit the Pause button on her Wikipedia playback. "Camel caravans once brought grain from—"

"There she is!" shouted Fiona, pointing to woman with flaming red hair who was wearing a long, flowing white gown.

"Let me do all the talking, guys," said Tommy.

We all nodded. He is the oldest.

"But if there's any wheeling and dealing to be done..." said Beck.

"I'll let you take over."

Beck handled a lot of the negotiating with merchants and vendors when we were on board *The Lost*. She was excellent at haggling. But this would be her first hostage negotiation.

CHAPTER 45

The six of us huddled in the cool shadows underneath one of the Khan's arches.

There was a group of tourists listening to a guide droning on in a dull monotone about how "Jazzar Pasha built this storage depot over parts of the Crusaders' port." He sounded even more boring than Storm. But he did remind us all why we were in Acre.

This was the port city where the Knights Templar stored their famous treasure.

"Your parents refused to cooperate with us," Fiona's mother told us. "They wouldn't lead us to the secret hiding place. We trust that you children, however, will."

"Oh, really?" said Tommy, puffing up his chest and trying to look tough. "And why do you think that's gonna happen, Dame Elizabeth, if that really is your name, which, in case you forgot, it isn't, Mrs. Amelia Glendenning!"

Fiona's mom look confused for a half second. She wasn't used to Tommy and his train of thought, which, sometimes, hops the tracks.

"Thomas, permit me to be as clear as I possibly can," said Mrs. Glendenning. "If you children don't find the treasure for us, you will force us to execute your mother and father." She stepped into the sunshine outside the arch and gazed up at the clock tower. "They will be burnt at the stake, just like the last Knights Templar were in France. You have twenty-four hours."

"To solve a centuries-old mystery?" blurted Beck, even though Tommy was supposed to be doing all the talking.

"I'm sure you children possess all the necessary skills and talents. Your parents keep telling us that you are quite clever and resourceful. After all, you did somehow manage to follow all the clues that led you here to Acre."

"Yeah," said Tommy, taking in a deep, satisfied breath. "It's true. We are pretty awesome. We did a lot of treasure hunting on our own without parental supervision back in the day. Did I ever tell you about the time the four of us were treasure hunting in China?"

"No, Thomas. You've never told me anything. We've never met, remember?"

"Riiiiight. Good point."

"Hang on," said Beck, who, I think, had lost her confidence in Tommy's ability to broker this deal to secure Mom and Dad's release. "Let's say we find the treasure for you. How do we know you'll free Mom and Dad? How do we know you won't hurt them?"

Dame Elizabeth curtsied slightly. "I giveth thee mine word of honor. And, as thou might knowest, it is against the code of chivalry for me to lieth."

"Muh-ther?" said Fiona. "Puh-leeze. You're not Shakespeare!"

Fiona's mom shot her a dirty look. "Very well.

Do you have your boyfriend's phone number?"

"He's not my—"

"I broke up with her," said Tommy.

"Exchange digits," commanded Dame Elizabeth. "Fiona will contact you later, Thomas, and bring you proof of life. A photograph of her posing with your parents."

Tommy and Fiona swapped phone numbers.

While they did, Storm narrowed her eyes and scrunched up her face. I could tell: something about Mrs. Glendenning and her daughter, Fiona, was bugging her.

"Come along, Fiona. Your father and I are looking forward to a nice family dinner this evening."

Fiona made a thumb-and-pinky phone, jiggling her hand next to her ear. "I'll call you, Tommy."

"Okay. But remember, our relationship is just like a flabby dude. It's not working out."

"This way," said Dame Elizabeth. She gave her flowing robe a good swish and sashayed away. Fiona, dutifully, followed her.

"We should shadow them!" I whispered. "Find

where they're keeping Mom and Dad! Execute a rescue plan!"

Dame Elizabeth whirled around. "And don't you dare follow us. My husband is standing by with a box of wooden matches. If I sense that we are being tailed, I will call him and your parents will perish in a roaring blaze!"

They disappeared in the darkness under the arches.

"I still say we should go after them!" I shouted.

"And I still say you're an idiot!" shouted Beck.

"No, I'm not! Dame Elizabeth knows where they've got Mom and Dad."

"Of course she knows!" screamed Beck. "She's one of the kidnappers. The kidnappers always know where they've stashed their kidnappees!"

Yep. Right there in the old open-air, camel-caravan warehouse, Beck and I launched into Twin Tirade number 2,046. That tourist group wandered over to see what all the screaming was about.

"We have to do something!" I shouted, not as loudly as I had at the start of the tirade.

Beck hollered back. She was running out of steam, too. "Mom always says something is better than nothing."

"I miss Mom. And Dad."

Beck nodded. "I miss 'em both."

"Yeah. Me, too."

"Of course you do."

"So, uh, what were we fighting about?"

CHAPTER 46

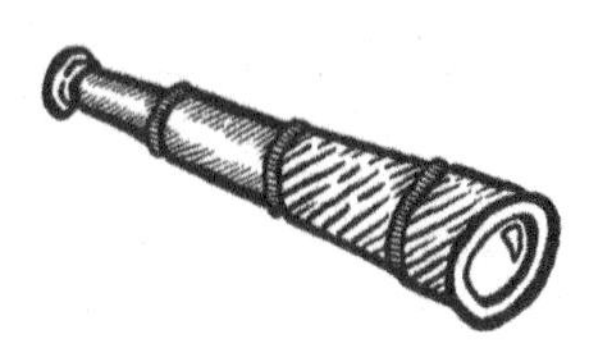

Storm let us all know what she was thinking.

"Did it look to any of you like Fiona and her mom haven't spoken in years?"

"Nope," I said. Tommy and Beck just shook their heads.

"And," said Storm, "if they haven't spoken in years, how come Fiona's mother has her own special ringtone?"

Tommy gasped. "She's been spying on us all along!"

Storm nodded slowly. "That's what I've been thinking. We don't share any information with Fiona. Let's not let her know that we know what we think we know."

"We can do that," I said.

"Yeah," said Beck. "Bick is really good at not knowing stuff."

"Takes one to not know one!" I shot back.

"Huh?"

"Never mind. It made sense in my brain. Until I said it."

"We should probably find a room for the night," said Tommy. "Some place to turn into our headquarters for this operation."

"There's a youth hostel called the Eco Akko, here in the Old City," said Storm, tapping her phone screen. "It's not too far from that Templar tunnel entrance I spotted off Asher Street. The hostel gets four-point-eight stars."

"Excellent," said Tommy.

We walked along the seawall. We would've been enjoying the warm sunshine and salty sea breeze if there wasn't a ticking time clock for us to find the Templar treasure. We had less than a day to do what others had been trying to do for more than seven centuries!

“I’m also going to need to use the laptop, Tommy,” said Storm. “We have to find a local to help us set up an underwater Wi-Fi system like we had on *The Lost*.”

“How come?” I wondered.

“You guys are going to need to do a little diving with the augmented reality masks,” said Storm, pointing to that curved cove where seawater was still crashing against huge rocks. “Remember, that’s where the treasure tower is. Well, where it used to be. Its base is still submerged under the sea. The tunnel will only take us so far. Then you guys will have to go for a swim. Go ahead. Put on the masks. Check it out.”

So, since we only had two dive masks left in a duffel bag (Uncle Sam had grabbed the other one back at the cafe), we fired up the laptop, and Beck, Tommy, and I took turns gazing out at the sea to see the scene that Storm had already seen.

We had an amazing augmented reality view of what once stood where we were currently standing. After Beck took her turn with the dive mask,

NOW:

THEN:

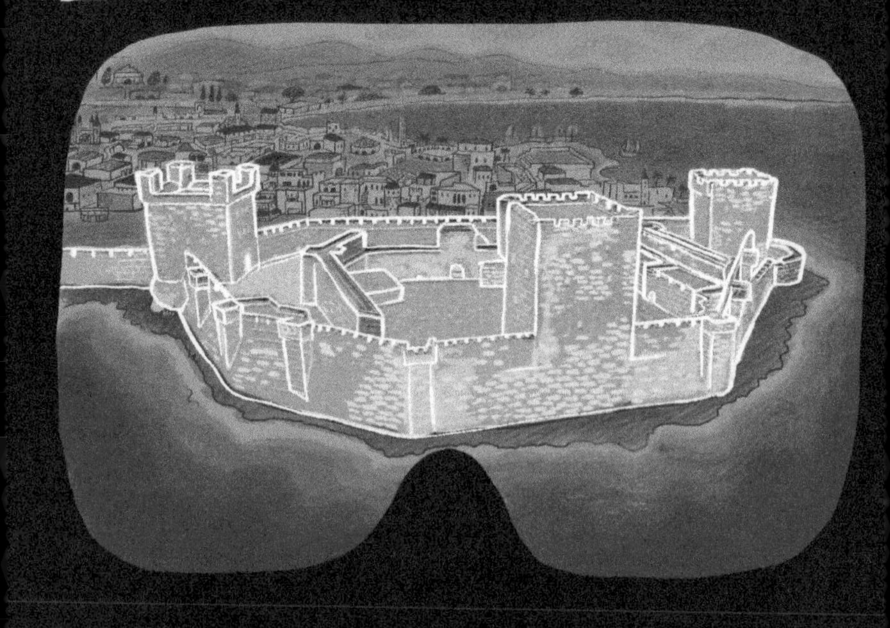

she quickly sketched a wider view of what was there now and what used to be there during the Crusades.

The "Now" drawing showed, basically, a rock-lined harbor ending at the seawall. The "Then" sketch showed a massive fortress squatting in that exact same spot. It was the Templars' final castle, complete with a blockhouse tower. According to all the data Mom and Dad had collected and compiled, the treasure we were looking for was down in the cellar of that stronghold. A cellar that was now several feet beneath the surface of the Mediterranean Sea!

CHAPTER 47

We booked our beds at the hostel, knowing we wouldn't be spending much time in them.

Then we carried our bags up to the roof deck, and Storm began her laptop search for what she called an Israeli techno geek, but what Beck and I called Storm's kindred spirit. That made Storm blush a little, but she didn't deny it.

"I found just the guy," she announced after a few hours of key clacking. "Ezra. His name means 'help and assistance' so, naturally, he's eager to lend a hand. He also liked my profile pic."

"How old is he?" asked Tommy.

"Same age as me."

"All right, all right," said Tommy.

Now Storm's ears were turning red. She quickly changed the subject. "Ezra's putting together an underwater Wi-Fi system that'll convert the standard wireless signal to one that can be transmitted optically via a 520-nanometer laser that it will beam to an optical receiver underwater with a high transfer speed."

We all nodded.

We had no idea what Ezra and Storm were cooking up.

We just hoped it would work.

Ezra would need several hours to build his gadget, Storm told us. But, as his final text assured her, he was "willing to work through the night for you, Stephanie." Yep. Storm had given the guy her real name.

"We should grab some shut-eye," said Tommy. "We'll head for the Templar tunnel before first light. If we're lucky, we can slip in, undetected."

"Good idea," I said, stretching into a yawn.

But sleep would have to wait.

Because Tommy's phone chirped. Fiona was calling.

CHAPTER 48

Fiona joined us under the stars up on the roof of the hostel where there were a bunch of tables and chairs.

"Why'd you bring your brother and sisters?" Fiona asked Tommy.

"Hey," said Tommy, "in case you forgot, my mom and dad are also their mom and dad."

"We'd all like to authenticate your proof-of-life photograph," said Storm, defiantly.

"Very well," said Fiona. "If you must..."

"We must," Beck and I said together.

Fiona pulled out her phone and thumbed open its camera app to show us a stark, brightly lit image.

"As you can see by the time stamp, I took this selfie with your mother and father less than an hour ago."

"They're both fine," Fiona said, trying to reassure us.

It didn't work.

We all started steaming the instant Fiona said they were "fine."

Sure, it was Mom and Dad. And Fiona was

wearing the same clothes in the shot as she was wearing now. The time and date stamp confirmed that it was, indeed, a very recent snapshot—not something the evil Glendenning family had posed a few days earlier.

That was the good news.

The bad news? Mom and Dad were blindfolded with their hands tied behind their backs. There was duct tape sealing their mouths.

We all shook our heads and gave Fiona our dirtiest, most disgusted looks.

"You still claim your parents aren't evil?" snapped Beck, speaking for all of us.

"They're just misguided," Fiona insisted.

"Nope," I said. "They're evil. Not to mention wicked, vile, and nasty!"

"I apologize for their rude behavior."

"Rude?" said Tommy. "Try criminal."

"I don't really care what you four think!" Now Fiona was the one fuming. "Family always comes first!"

"Even when they're wackaloons?" I asked.

"They're not bad people!" Fiona insisted again.

"Uh, yeah," said Beck. "We think they might be."

Furious, Fiona shook her head. "No! They're just exhibiting bad judgment and bad behavior."

"Chya," said Tommy. "Like, the worst judgment and behavior ever."

"I just want to put my family back together," said Fiona. "It's the most important treasure in the world."

"We agree," I said. "Too bad your family has been trying to tear our family apart!"

"Look," said Fiona, sounding almost as exasperated with us as we were with her. "Find the treasure, and this will all be over. I promise. Your mom and dad will be fine."

"Where are they?" asked Storm.

"I can't tell you. But, in a sign of good faith and to show their noble intentions, my parents gave me a riddle to share with you guys."

"Is it the one about the bowling ball?" asked Tommy. "Because that one's extremely difficult..."

"I didn't look at the riddle." She handed

Tommy an envelope. "They said it was for your eyes only."

"And for you to look at it would break the code of chivalry," I said, sounding super bored. "Yadda, yadda, yadda."

Fiona ignored me. "They'll give you more information about precisely where to find your parents right after you text me the location of the Templar treasure. After that text, Tommy, we'll never see or hear from each other again."

Tommy shrugged. "Works for me. Like I said, we need to become better strangers."

Fiona handed Tommy the riddle envelope, turned on her heel, and left the hostel's rooftop garden in a huff.

"Well done, Tommy," said Storm.

"Yeah," said Beck. "Finally, you didn't give one of your girlfriends the chance to double-cross us!"

"Read the riddle!" I said.

Tommy ripped open the envelope and gave us the puzzle that, according to Fiona, would help us locate Mom and Dad:

I have a deck but no backyard
I have a bow but no arrows
I have a wheel but I'm not a car
I have a beam but I'm not a light
I have a stern but I'm not serious
I have a crow's nest but there are no birds

To which, I wanted to say: "I have a feeling this is the easiest riddle ever written!"

CHAPTER 49

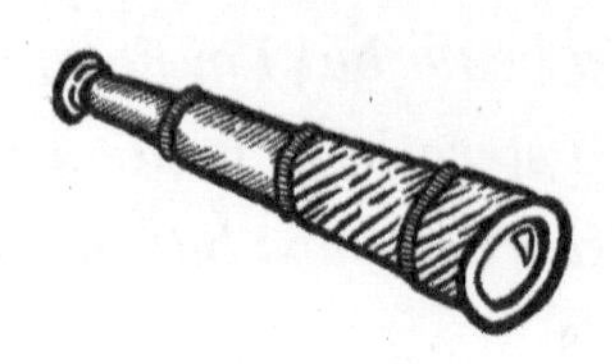

"They're on a boat," we all said together.

I added a "Duh."

Hey, a first grader could've solved that riddle. Maybe even a kindergartener.

But which boat? There were hundreds docked in the port city's many marinas.

"Let's search them all!" said Tommy.

"We don't have time," I reminded him. "The clock is ticking."

"Bick's right," said Beck. "We have to give these 'new Knights Templar' what they want. All that magnificent, incredible, unbelievably valuable treasure."

“I agree,” I said. “Mom and Dad are worth more than all the treasures in the world!”

“True,” said Storm. “But first we have to find it. That tunnel will lead us into the old Crusader city that still exists beneath modern-day Acre. The data Mom and Dad gathered for the augmented reality dive masks should guide us into and under that cove where the Templars’ treasure tower used to stand.”

Storm made a quick sketch on the back of the riddle envelope. It wasn’t as good as Beck’s drawing would’ve been, but it did the job.

“Previewing the material,” said Storm, “I’m confident that a hidden room at the base of that tower is the treasure chamber Dad and Mom had discovered. But there is another room beneath that chamber.”

“The basement has a basement?” said Tommy.

“Exactly!”

“So, what’s in the lower chamber?” I asked.

“A deep cistern filled with rainwater,” says Storm. “The Crusaders stockpiled an enormous pool of fresh water in case there was ever a siege and they were cut off from the river and their other sources of drinking water. But we need to be careful. I suspect that sealed-up water is under enormous pressure so they could quickly pump it up to the surface in an emergency. So, whatever you guys do, when you enter the treasure chamber, do not, I repeat, do not turn any valves or open any hatches that might lead to that lower chamber!"

"What happens if we do?" asked Beck.

"KABOOM!" said Storm, flicking open her fingers to indicate fireworks. "It'll be like a geyser. And, trust me, nobody should go scuba diving in a geyser."

We all returned to our rolled-out mattresses in the hostel and grabbed a few hours of sleep.

Well, I mostly had nightmares about being bounced around on top of Old Faithful, the geyser in Yellowstone National Park that, as the name implies, erupts on a very regular basis, shooting thousands of gallons of four-hundred-degree water 180 feet in the sky.

Around five a.m., we packed up our gear and hiked over to the Templar tunnel entrance. Storm's new online Israeli techno-nerd friend, Ezra, met us there. He had really come through for us. Not only did he have the underwater Wi-Fi gizmo he and Storm designed, he'd also been able to scrounge up three scuba tanks, complete with regulator mouthpieces.

"Wow!" he said. "You guys really are the Kidds! I've read all about you in *Nerd Monthly* magazine."

(Yes. We do have our fans.)

Storm wiggle-waggled her eyebrows at Ezra. "I wish I were cross-eyed," she said, "so I could see you twice."

Storm was trying her best to sound like Tommy, and it seemed like it was working. The delighted Ezra was nervously laughing through his nose.

"I've got all the gear we discussed, Stephanie," Ezra said when he finally composed himself. "My uncle Shlomo runs a dive shop. Convenient, huh?

Hey, are you guys going on an actual treasure hunt? Right now? Is that why you needed the scuba gear, too?"

"That's right, Ezra," said Tommy, giving the guy one of his manly winks.

"This is so awesome! Can I come with you? Can I be like an honorary Kidd Family Treasure Hunter for a day?"

"Of course," said Storm. "We wouldn't be able to find this particular treasure without you and your incredible underwater Wi-Fi system!"

"Then I'm glad I brought it!" Ezra hoisted a gym bag and gave us another nose-snort laugh. "And the scuba stuff, too!"

We grabbed our dive gear bags and the oxygen tanks.

And then, making sure nobody was watching, Storm led the way down into the Templar tunnel!

CHAPTER 50

Surprisingly, the tunnel was extremely well lit for, you know, a secret subterranean passage-way.

Tommy opened the laptop and powered it on.

“Guess if the battery dies,” said Storm, “we could recharge it by plugging it into one of those wall outlets!”

“Storm?” I said. “I thought this tunnel was supersecret inside information.”

“Oh, no,” said Ezra with a snorty chuckle. “This is one of Acre’s biggest tourist attractions. People come down here all the time. It was discov-ered back in 1994.”

"So, Mom and Dad's top secret data is, like, common knowledge?" said Tommy.

"Yes," said Storm. "But only this 150-meter stretch of the tunnel. There are also secret tunnels."

"Really?" said Ezra. "Where are they?"

Storm actually winked at the guy. "You'll see."

She put on one of the augmented reality masks, established a link with Tommy's open laptop, and, following the overlapping grid of the ancient city of Acre projected on the mask's glass, led us farther down the tunnel.

"There was a guardhouse right here," she reported. "Only true Knights Templar with special permission could move on to the treasure tower."

"Is it at the end of the tunnel?" I asked.

Storm shook her head. "Nope. It's through this wall."

"Huh?" said Ezra. "That's not very smart tunnel design. How do you walk through a wall?"

"Well, according to Mom and Dad's notes, by

playing it music." Storm raised the dive mask, found her phone, and clicked on the music app.

A familiar angelic melody poured out of her speakers.

"I recorded this when we were downstairs at the Rosslyn Chapel," she said. "It's that thirteen-note Rosslyn Motet."

Once again, a stone in the wall started to shimmy and shake. It quivered its way forward, pulling itself out of the wall.

"This is how we found that other secret entrance!" said Tommy.

We all pressed our shoulders against the stone and slid it aside.

We'd opened a narrow doorway into a dark tunnel.

"This is definitely not on any of the tunnel maps I've ever seen," said Ezra. "Who knew it was even here?"

I grinned. "Our mom and dad. The smartest treasure hunters on earth."

"Come on," said Tommy, holding up his

illuminated phone and leading the way into the darkness.

The stone floor had a steep slant.

After about ten yards, our feet started slapping water. At first, it was just a puddle. Pretty soon, it was up over our ankles.

"This passageway will keep slanting downward until, in another twenty yards, it'll burrow underneath that rocky cove where the fortress once stood," Storm explained. "I suspect that section of the tunnel will be flooded. It's time for you guys to suit up while Ezra and I activate the underwater Wi-Fi to beam you the augmented reality information you're going to need to find and enter the treasure tower."

"Suit up, team!" said Tommy.

"This is going to work!" I shouted.

Beck added a "Woo-hoo!"

We quickly unzipped the gear bags and started tugging our wet suits on over our clothes.

Tommy, of course, was two steps ahead of me and Beck. He was already securing his AR mask when Beck and I reached into the duffel to grab ours.

Except there was only one left.

Because of Uncle Sam. Remember? He'd angrily snatched a mask away from Storm at that cafe, and he didn't give it back.

"I should go," I said.

"Why?" said Beck.

"Because I'm older than you."

"By one minute!"

"So? A minute counts. It's sixty whole seconds!"

This was not a Twin Tirade. This was an actual argument. We both wanted to be the one joining Tommy on this last leg of the treasure quest. What can I say? Treasure questing is in our DNA!

"You guys?" said Tommy, holding up a gloved hand to silence us. "Pop quiz. Dead on the field lie ten soldiers in white, felled by three eyes, black as night. What happened?"

"Um, the Knights Templar fought a dragon with three eyes!" blurted Beck.

SERIOUSLY, BECK? YOU MADE ME LOOK LIKE A FROG?

YOU WON THE RIDDLE; I WON THE DRAWING.

"Nope. Bick?"

"Um, a bowling ball knocked over all ten pins?"

"Correct. Grab a mask, Bick. We've got some diving to do."

CHAPTER 51

Tommy and I kept walking down the sloping stone ramp.

We had our wet suits on and scuba tanks strapped to our backs. We'd adjusted our regulators and were breathing nice and easy, even though my heart was starting to beat a little faster.

Because we were about to swim into a chamber where, if Mom and Dad were correct, one of the greatest treasures of all time was just sitting waiting for us to find it!

"Turn on the AR masks!" Storm shouted.

Tommy and I both gave her a thumbs-up and activated the augmented reality interface. The glass on our dive masks became a flickering video game display, showing a greenish, crisscrossing grid image of what used to be where we were right now.

Soon, the water was up to our hips. Then our chests. Finally, it was over our heads.

We were fully submerged. The instant we were underwater in the flooded tunnel, the graphic imagery on our dive mask screens disappeared. It was like a phone shutting down. Two seconds later, the architectural imagery was back! Ezra's underwater Wi-Fi rig was working.

Tommy gave me an arm chop signal.

He saw something up ahead.

A doorway.

The water pressure on each side of it was so intense, it took both of us leaning against the wood and straining and grunting (which is hard to do when you're breathing through a mouthpiece) to get it to budge. But once it had a little inertia, it swung open.

And banged into a skeleton!

The limp bag of bones tumbled in slow motion to the floor of the underwater corridor.

The bony-faced guy was dressed in full Knights Templar chain mail. His white robe with the red templar cross was ragged and torn, like fish had been nibbling on it for centuries. His skeletal hand clutched a sword. His whole body bobbed up and down as it slowly settled to the floor. A wormy sea creature squirmed out of an eyehole in his skull.

Gingerly swimming over the seven-hundred-year-old corpse, we kept moving forward.

It was almost as if we were back in that lost city

submerged off the coast of Egypt. The data stream kept coming. Now the archaeological architecture grid was pointing out interesting landmarks. A tunnel leading off to the armory. Another tunnel leading to the chapel. And, just up ahead, a passage labeled APSCONDITUM ARQUITIS.

Suddenly, Tommy made a gesture for me to swim down so my belly was on the floor.

Now!

We both did.

Right before a barrage of crusty, rusty arrows came shooting out of the side walls from some kind of medieval speargun. Apparently, stepping on that loose stone had triggered a Knights Templar booby trap!

Fortunately, Tommy had been a better Latin student than me during our Classic Languages classes with Dad on board *The Lost*. He knew that *apsconditum arquitis* translated into "hidden archers."

Once past that little death trap, the flooded corridor came to a room with three separate exits. The info on our mask screens told us to take the one in the center. And, finally, when we came to the next split in the underwater maze, the mask data told us to head right.

Which we did, until we came to a dead end.

A stone wall.

With what looked like a rusty cast-iron ring bolted into it.

Following the instructions printed on our glass screens, Tommy and I took hold of the ring and twisted it counterclockwise.

All of a sudden, the water in the flooded corridor started to gush down a drain and whoosh away. It was as if someone had pulled out the stopper in a stone-lined bathtub.

When the waterline receded to waist level, Tommy took out his regulator, turned to me, and said, "It must be an airlock of some kind. Man, this water is draining away fast."

I checked out the floor. Several storm grates were now visible. Two minutes later, the whole passageway was empty and nearly dry. The only water left was the droplets trickling off our dive suits and the wet sheen on the stones.

"Where'd all that water go?" I wondered.

Tommy shrugged. "Out to sea, I guess. Come on. Give me a hand."

We grabbed the ring and pulled the stone open as if it were a door because, hello, it was!

A door into the Knights Templar's subterranean treasure trove!

Yep. We'd found it!

CHAPTER 52

It was a good thing that Tommy and I both had oxygen tanks.

Otherwise, we might've lost our breath.

The Knights Templar's treasure horde was definitely breathtaking! We're talking a mountain of gold, jewelry, precious artifacts, and glittering gewgaws. It climbed in a mound thirty, maybe forty feet tall right in front of us. We shone our dive lights up, up, up until we reached the glittering summit.

We tilted back our dive masks and gawked up at the monumental, not to mention colossal, heap of precious objects.

"Soak it in, little brother," said Tommy. "We're probably the first humans to see this loot since those Crusaders stashed it down here seven or eight hundred years ago. Probably why it smells a little musty in here. Like a damp basement with a busted sump pump."

"When do we have Storm text Fiona?" I asked. "When do we let the Glendennings know we've met their ransom demands?"

"In a minute," said Tommy, sighing. "I kind of hate to say buh-bye to all this booty."

"We're exchanging it for Mom and Dad, Tommy. That's the ultimate treasure."

"Yeah. I know. I just wish there was a way to have both. Mom and Dad and all this Templar treasure."

"Unfortunately, you'll be getting neither!" boomed a voice behind us.

Suddenly, the chamber was filled with bright light that made the plunder tower even more dazzling. It also made us blind when we whipped our heads around. All we could see was a brilliant beacon beaming right at our eyeballs. I held up my arm to block the light and could make out several silhouettes.

One was definitely Beck. Another was Storm.

I think a third shadow was her new Israeli boyfriend, Ezra.

"Well done, Kidds," said the voice, stepping forward as some of the searchlights were lowered.

It was Uncle Sam and his whole CIA crew. Sam was wearing the dive mask he'd basically stolen from us at the cafe. His goon squad had their weapons trained on Storm and Beck.

But not Ezra.

Wait a second, I thought. Did Storm's boyfriend just double-cross her the way Tommy's girlfriends usually double-crossed him on our adventures?

"Thank you so much for draining the tunnels," said Sam, tossing his AR dive mask to one of his flunkies. "Your parents' data stream proved quite useful as well." He wagged his finger at Tommy and me. "You children should've told me about this fantastic treasure-hunting software housed in your laptop."

"That's proprietary information!" shouted Beck. "Property of Kidd Family Treasure Hunters and intended for the sole and private use of those attempting to rescue our parents!"

"Sorry, little lady. We have bigger fish to fry." Uncle Sam stepped forward, swung up his halogen lantern beam, and admired the unbelievable treasure trove in front of him. "Certain very important people on the Arabian peninsula need their treasure returned to them in exchange for permission to build a new air base on their sovereign territory. All right, team. Set up the work lights. Initiate the calls. It's time to organize the extraction crew. But first, let me snap a few photos to share with our influential friends. I am sure they will be pleased."

I raised my hand to ask a question.

"Yes, Bickford?" said Uncle Sam. "Question?"

"Yeah. Was Ezra working for you guys all along?"

"Of course I was," said Ezra. "How else do you think I could come up with all the electronic gear you people needed to concoct your cockamamie underwater Wi-Fi system, which, somehow actually worked? That was all these guys, not me. And scuba tanks? Give me a break. Where did you think I found those in the middle of the night?"

"From your Uncle Shlomo," I said. "The one who runs a dive shop."

"Uncle Shlomo is the code name I use when operating in Israel," said Uncle Sam.

"I feel so betrayed," said Storm, sounding more sad than angry.

"I know the feeling, sis," said Tommy. "Comes with the territory."

"What territory?"

"Looking as awesome as we do."

"We're all sorry, of course, about the loss of your parents," said Uncle Sam.

"Excuse me?" I said.

"I know you children were hoping to exchange this treasure for your parents' release from those screwball Knights Templar wannabes."

"Uh, yeah," said Beck. "That's been the plan all along."

"Well, unfortunately, that's not gonna happen, Rebecca. Sorry about that. But sometimes we all have to make sacrifices for the greater good."

"Like right now!" shouted a new voice as two dozen more people came charging into the treasure chamber. "That treasure is ours!"

Among them was Dame Elizabeth and ten other knuckleheads wearing armor covered in white tunics with red crosses emblazoned on their chests. One of them was Fiona! Storm had been correct. Fiona had been a spy for her parents all along and had been stringing us along, hoping, like Uncle Sam, that we'd find the treasure for her and her team!

They all raised their swords.

Even Fiona.

The new Knights Templar had arrived to lay siege to the old knights' fortress.

CHAPTER 53

The CIA guys raised their weapons as the new Knights raised theirs.

"It's like 1291 all over again!" shouted Storm, referring, of course, to the Siege of Acre when the Crusaders (and the original Knights Templar) lost control of this port city to the Mamluk Sultanate. Of course, back then, neither side had semi-automatic weapons.

"Stand down, Knight Hugo!" shouted Uncle Sam, raising his pistol with both hands.

"No!" Fiona's father shouted back. "You stand down."

Uncle Sam shook his head. "No, you!"

"I said it first!"

"No, you did not. I did!"

"This is our treasure!" declared Dame Elizabeth.

"And we shall reclaim it by any means necessary!" cried Fiona, who had gone full new Knight nutty on us. She brandished a broadsword over her head. "The family that slays together, stays together!"

"This isn't the Middle Ages, Fiona," replied Uncle Sam. "And in the great game of rock, paper, scissors—semiautomatic pistol beats sword every time."

"Nuh-uh!" sneered Knight Hugo, who seemed too totally immature to be Sir Anything. "We're wearing armor. So, bullets bounce off breastplate but sword slices through safari jacket."

"Prepareth to meet thy maker!" screamed Fiona, kissing the hilt of her sword like, I think, Joan of Arc used to do. Oh, yeah. Fiona had definitely signed up for whatever harebrained alternate reality her parents had decided to live in. She even sounded like her mom.

"Wait," said Uncle Sam, lowering his weapon in a sign of good faith. "I'm willing to make a deal."

"A deal?" said Knight Hugo.

"Yes. There's plenty of treasure here. More than enough to satisfy our 'clients.' We could negotiate an arrangement to make everybody happy and avoid any kind of...injuries."

"A most noble notion," said Fiona's dad. "After all, the original Knights Templar were banking pioneers and financial wizards. They understoodeth the art of the deal."

"Good," said Uncle Sam. "But first, one question—how'd you people find this treasure trove so easily?"

"Simple," said Fiona. "Once I had Tommy's number, all I had to do was track his phone and, thereby, his movements."

"Nertz," muttered Tommy. "I should've put it on airplane mode."

"And then, good sir," Fiona continued with a curtsy to Uncle Sam, "we followed you and your team as you followed Tommy and Bick."

"But I broke up with you!" Tommy protested.

"You were supposed to immediately delete my digits. It's in the modern code of chivalry."

"Sorry," said Fiona with a shrug. "I prefereth the olden code."

"Is it okay if I leave now?" asked Ezra. "I've kind of done my job with the underwater Wi-Fi and—"

"No one leaveth here until this deal hath been sealed!" boomed Fiona's scary mom.

"Right," said Ezra, holding up both hands and taking a few steps backward. "Gotcha. Just curious..."

"How about we give you twenty percent of everything in that pile?" said Uncle Sam. "You guys can have all the crowns and swords and goblets. We mostly want the gold and jewels."

"Thirty percent!" countered Dame Elizabeth.

"Twenty-five!" said Uncle Sam.

"We must hurry, Dame Elizabeth," said Knight Hugo. "Our ship has been rigged for arson and will be ablaze in..."

He checked his wristwatch, which, if you ask

me, is a weird thing for a knight to do.

"Twenty-three minutes. It would be best if we were long gone before the authorities start investigating the death of Dr. and Mrs. Kidd on board our flaming yacht."

"What?!?" the four of us shouted.

"Poetic justice," said Dame Elizabeth. "We have your very uncooperative and unhelpful mother and father lashed to the mast of our sailboat. We have set up an incendiary device on a timer. When it goes off in twenty-three—"

"Twenty-two," said her husband.

"Twenty-two minutes, it will ignite a fire. Dr. and Mrs. Kidd will burn at the stake and suffer the same fate Jacques de Molay, the last grand master of the Knights Templar, did in 1314!"

"But you promised us!" shouted Beck. "If we gave you the Templar treasure as ransom, you'd release our parents."

"You lied!" I screamed. "That's against your code of chivalry!"

"We did not lie!" proclaimed Dame Elizabeth.

"For you did not 'give' us the Templar treasure. We found it ourselves!"

"Chya," said Tommy. "By following us!"

Dame Elizabeth grinned a wickedly sinister grin. "Because we are extremely clever. And our daughter is even more cunning." She turned to face Uncle Sam. "We accept your offer, good sir. Twenty-five percent is agreeable. Let us hurry forth and divvy up the spoils."

"Wait!" demanded Storm, who'd been quietly shooting eye-daggers at Ezra. "What about our parents?"

"They, I'm happy to say, will soon meet their maker!"

"In twenty-one minutes," added Knight Hugo, checking his wristwatch again. "Sorry. Twenty minutes."

This was a nightmare! We needed a new plan.

Fast.

I looked around the treasure chamber. It was very well lit now, thanks to all the portable halogen lamps Uncle Sam's team had dragged in with them.

There had to be some way out of this.

Some bargaining chip to offer the evil Glendennings in exchange for Mom and Dad's location.

And then I saw it.

On the floor.

It looked like a rust-covered, cast-iron version of a ship wheel.

And, if Storm was correct (which she usually is), it could be exactly what we needed to keep our family together!

CHAPTER 54

"Wait!" I shouted. "This isn't all the treasure."

"What?" hissed Fiona's mother.

"Come again?" said Uncle Sam.

"Mom and Dad were being greedy," I told my audience of knights, dames, and spies. I made a sweeping arm gesture, pointing to the shimmering mountain behind me. "This room is only the first of the twin Templar treasure chambers. For, as good bankers, they knew you should never put all your eggs in one basket or all your gold, jewels, and precious knickknacks in one heap. Mom and Dad did not put the location of that second, even bigger room in our laptop computer's archaeological database for fear that the information would fall into the wrong hands."

"But," said Beck, jumping in to help out (it's another one of those twin things), "they told us where to find it!"

"They did?" said Tommy innocently. "Huh."

"Yes, Tommy," I said. "They told me and Beck. They knew we would not divulge that secret information to anyone, not even our older brother and sister. For we have a code far stronger than the code of chivalry. It's called..."

I took one of Beck's hands. She clasped it tight. We raised our joined hands high and proclaimed together, "The Twin Code!"

"Of course," said Storm, catching on to what we were up to. "Why, the Twin Code goes all the way back to Romulus and Remus, the twin brothers responsible for the founding of Ancient Rome!"

"Exactly!" I said.

Then, I narrowed my eyes and glared at Dame Elizabeth.

"We twins shalt reveal the secret we share

to thee as soon as thou shalt tell us where thou docked thy sailboat. You give us that location and we'll give you the location of the second Treasure Vault!"

"Do it," urged Uncle Sam. "There'll be so much treasure, we can all dip our beaks and pocket a little for ourselves."

Dame Elizabeth thought about my proposition for maybe two seconds.

"Fine. Your mother and father are very close by. The Akko Marina. Berth 23. If you hurry, you might be able to save their wretched lives."

The four of us were ready to bolt.

"Aren't you Kidd kids forgetting something?" said Uncle Sam, raising his pistol ever so slightly.

"Right. Sorry. Time crunch."

I pointed to the big iron wheel on the floor.

"This basement to the treasure tower has a sub-basement. Just turn that big valve to open the floor hatch and gain access to the room below. According to what Mom and Dad told us, there's twice as much treasure down there than there is up here."

"En-joy!" said Beck, waving buh-bye.

The four of us flicked on our phone flashlights and dashed out of the room.

"Come on!" I heard Uncle Sam say. "Get over here. Lend a hand, you knights."

We were tearing up the tunnel, retracing our steps in reverse order as quickly as we could. The screeching squeal of the rusty wheel was so loud, it echoed up the arched stone corridors.

"Faster, you guys!" shouted Tommy, who must've activated the timer on his dive watch. "We only have fifteen more minutes before that sailboat explodes and fries Mom and Dad!"

"Why'd you tell them to turn that wheel, Bick?" asked Storm, as we huffed and puffed up that final slanted pathway leading to the hidden stone portal—the rock we opened with sympathetic vibrations with the Rosslyn Motet. "That's most likely the valve to the cistern below. Do you know how dangerous that much water under that much pressure can be?"

"Yeah," I said. "I kind of do. Especially after I'm pretty sure Tommy and I added about a million more gallons to it when we drained the corridors."

"This way!" said Beck, pointing to a ladder bolted to the wall. It led to a manhole cover in the street.

I clambered up first. Storm was after me. Then Beck. Then Tommy.

We were panting hard when we reached the surface.

"There!" said Storm, pointing to dozens of boats moored between floating docks. "That's the Akko Marina. We need to find Berth 23!"

I don't think any of us have ever run that fast before.

But then we heard something that made us stop in our tracks.

A big VA-VOOM followed by a roaring gush of water.

"Guess they finally got it open," said Storm. "And look, there's Ezra!"

CHAPTER 55

We allowed ourselves thirty seconds to survey the scene behind us.

There, in that cove where the Templars' fortress once stood, was a gushing geyser. A volcanic eruption of white water shooting up ten, twenty, thirty feet. Inside the cloud of sea spray, I could see a soaked Ezra bouncing up and down. A dazed and drenched Uncle Sam looked like he was in the spin cycle. There was also a floundering Fiona and both her waterlogged, doggy-paddling parents. They, and the rest of the treasure-stealing crew of knights, ladies, and CIA agents, were being buffeted up by the unbelievably powerful

WOOSH!

EVERYONE'S FAVORITE WEATHER FORECAST:

IT'S **RAINING** TREASURE.

blast of high-pressure water they'd just released. It's like they were bodysurfing in a cloud.

"Nooooo!" I heard Dame Elizabeth scream as she splash-landed in the sea.

Because all that ancient Knights Templar treasure was now raining down like pennies from heaven.

All the bad guys were in the water now, splashing and thrashing around as coins and candlesticks and goblets and jewelry tumbled out of the sky.

"Salvage it!" I heard Uncle Sam gurgle to his troops. "Save the treasure!"

"Grab as much as you can, Fiona!" cried her mother.

"You only get twenty-five percent!" screamed Uncle Sam.

"That deal is off!" Dame Elizabeth screamed back.

Everyone scrambled, pushed, and shoved—trying to clutch as much of the plummeting loot as they could. But the blast area was wide. Some of the treasure trickled down on the streets of

Acre where surprised and happy citizens scooped it up with glee.

We quit gawking at the treasure shower, leapt over a small wall, and scrambled up a floating dock.

"Twenty-three is all the way at the end!" I shouted.

"I can see Mom and Dad!" added Beck.

"Where?" said Storm.

"The mainmast. Up near the bow!"

"I see 'em," said Tommy, pumping his arms and churning his legs. He was chugging like a locomotive, bringing his knees up to his elbows with every stride.

Mom and Dad squirmed a little. They could see us coming.

They couldn't shout for joy because their mouths were still duct-taped.

"Why didn't somebody go rescue them?" asked Beck between gasps for breath.

"The sail," I said, panting heavily. "It blocks the view from land. You can only see them once you're down here on the dock."

Tommy leapt on board the sailboat.

"Sorry about this," I heard him say.

Then I heard the unmistakably painful RIIIIIIP of heavy silver tape being torn off face flesh.

"Thanks, Tommy!" said Dad.

"Thanks to all of you!" added Mom as the rest of us bounded on board the ship.

"One minute!" said Tommy.

This time, he wasn't tapping his watch. He gestured toward the digital readout on the fire bomb as it counted down to zero and the BA-BOOM that would follow. The device was at the base of the mainmast. Inches away from Mom and Dad's feet.

"Undo the knots, guys," said Tommy.

Good thing we're all excellent sailors. We can tie and untie knots like nobody's business.

We freed Mom and Dad's hands first.

Then, with their help, we worked on the ankle ropes.

"Thirty seconds!" shouted Tommy.

Mom and Dad shook free from the post.

"Into the water!" shouted Dad. "Everybody!"

"Including you, Storm!" added Mom.

"Yes, Mother," said Storm.

And then, even though she hates the water, Storm dove off the boat first. We all quickly followed and swam as far away from that ticking time bomb of a sailboat as we could.

But, when the device detonated, we heard the roar of the explosion and felt the blast of heat against the back of our heads.

Safe, we all treaded water and turned around to watch yet another sailboat erupt into a ball of black smoke and roiling flames as it slowly sank into the Mediterranean Sea.

CHAPTER 56

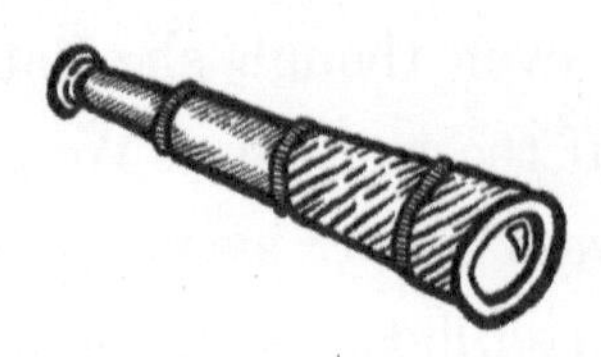

Gold coins and bullion bars were still falling from the sky.

Diamonds, emeralds, rubies, and sapphires, too.

A jewel-encrusted chalice nearly conked Tommy on the head.

We were all still in the water, swimming in place, and dodging the shimmering shower from the cloud of treasure sent skyward when Uncle Sam and the new Knights Templar opened up that highly pressurized reservoir of drinking water that Storm had warned us about.

"Got it!" said Mom, clutching a tumbling diamond out of the sky the way some people can snag a fly ball without a glove.

Dad laughed. "I always knew that, if we used our wits, our smarts, and worked together, we'd find the lost Templar treasure!"

"Ah, who needs it?" said Mom, flinging away the diamond she'd just barehanded. "We have our family. And that's the greatest treasure of all!"

We hung around the port city for another week.

We bought a new ship and started outfitting it for treasure hunting. It had even more gadgets and gizmos than we used to have on *The Lost*. Dad promised that it'd have more secret compartments, too.

We had some heated family discussions about what to christen our new craft but, in the end, the decision was unanimous.

Not *The Lost II*.

Nope.

Welcome aboard *The Lost Again*.

Several agents from Mossad, the Israeli intelligence agency, dropped by Acre to "round up and deal with" Uncle Sam (or as they knew him, "Uncle Shlomo"). They were very interested in the deal he had tried to broker with certain Saudi sheiks.

The State Department disavowed any knowledge of Mr. Samuel Heenehan's unsanctioned actions. The rest of his crew, we were told, were being put on desk duty back home in Virginia.

Fiona, her mother, and her father were spending some quiet time at one of the finest mental health institutes in the State of Israel, where they were undergoing a rigorous psychiatric evaluation. Some of the knights in their brigade were sentenced to months of community service in Acre. They'd be Knights Templar reenactors for all the tourists visiting that very popular tunnel.

Local authorities, along with ships from the Israeli navy, began dragging the floor of Acre harbor for all that scattered treasure. Their nets brought up loads of gold and precious artifacts, all of which would be put on exhibit in an Israeli museum. Any locals who found treasure on the streets were allowed to keep it.

As for us? We were ready to sail on to our next adventure.

Maybe we'd try to find the missing Florentine

Diamond. With 133 carats, it's the largest pink gem of its type in the world. Then there's the missing manuscript to a Shakespeare play called *Love's Labors Won,* a sequel to his *Love's Labors Lost,* that no one has seen or read since the 1600s. And, while in jolly old England, we could also go hunting for the missing jewels of King John.

"I just hope, wherever we go, I don't run into another Ezra," said Storm.

When she said that, Tommy put a comforting hand on her shoulder. "You will, sis. I'm afraid, for us, there will always be another Fiona and another Ezra. It's the just the price we have to pay."

"For being so gosh-darn attractive?"

"Exactly, Storm. Exactly."

"You guys?" called Mom.

She and Dad came up from belowdecks carrying our (brand-new) tablet computer. "It's a video call from Uncle Richie! He just finished up down in Antarctica. Say hello."

The four of us huddled around the screen.

"Hello, Uncle Richie!" Beck and I shouted.

Storm smiled. Tommy waved at the screen.

Uncle Richie waved back. He looked as jolly as ever. In fact, his new bushy beard made him look even jollier. "Hello to all of you! How are my favorite children in the whole wide world?"

"Fine, Uncle Richie," said Storm.

"Bully, Stephanie. Bully. Sorry I've been off the grid and incommunicado, as they say. Not many Wi-Fi hot spots ringing the South Pole. So, tell me: did I miss anything?"

We all just smiled.

"Not really, Uncle Richie," I said. "Just the same-old, same-old."

When I said that, everybody laughed—including Uncle Richie.

THE TREASURE HUNTERS SERIES

TREASURE HUNTERS

(with Chris Grabenstein)

The Kidds are not your normal family, traveling the world on crazy adventures to recover lost treasure. But when their parents disappear, Bick and his brother and sisters are thrown into the biggest (and most dangerous) treasure hunt of their lives.

DANGER DOWN THE NILE

(with Chris Grabenstein)

Bick, Beck, Storm and Tommy are navigating their way down the Nile, from a hot and dusty Cairo to deep dark jungles, past some seriously bad guys along the way.

SECRET OF THE FORBIDDEN CITY

(with Chris Grabenstein)

The Kidds are desperately trying to secure the ancient Chinese artefact that will buy their mother's freedom from kidnapping pirates.

PERIL AT THE TOP OF THE WORLD

(with Chris Grabenstein)

When the biggest heist in history takes place in Moscow, the Kidds rush in to save the day – but instead, they're accused of being the thieves themselves!

QUEST FOR THE CITY OF GOLD

(with Chris Grabenstein)

The Kidd family discovers an ancient map to a lost Incan City. But when the map is stolen, the Kidds have to navigate the dangerous Amazon jungle to locate the fabled city . . . before the bad guys find it first.

ALL-AMERICAN ADVENTURE

(with Chris Grabenstein)

The Kidds are stuck in Washington, DC without any priceless antiques to hunt. BORING! But everything changes when they uncover a dastardly conspiracy: a fake Bill of Rights!

THE PLUNDER DOWN UNDER

(with Chris Grabenstein)

While hunting for Lasseter's Gold, one of the legendary lost treasures of Australia, the Kidds' ship is waylaid by pirate Charlotte Badger, and the Kidds' parents are framed for stealing a set of priceless gems!

ALSO BY JAMES PATTERSON

MIDDLE SCHOOL SERIES

The Worst Years of My Life (*with Chris Tebbetts*)
Get Me Out of Here! (*with Chris Tebbetts*)
My Brother Is a Big, Fat Liar (*with Lisa Papademetriou*)
How I Survived Bullies, Broccoli, and Snake Hill (*with Chris Tebbetts*)
Ultimate Showdown (*with Julia Bergen*)
Save Rafe! (*with Chris Tebbetts*)
Just My Rotten Luck (*with Chris Tebbetts*)
Dog's Best Friend (*with Chris Tebbetts*)
Escape to Australia (*with Martin Chatterton*)
From Hero to Zero (*with Chris Tebbetts*)
Born to Rock (*with Chris Tebbetts*)
Master of Disaster (*with Chris Tebbetts*)
Field Trip Fiasco (*with Chris Tebbetts*)
It's a Zoo in Here! (*with Brian Sitts*)

ALI CROSS SERIES

Ali Cross
Ali Cross: Like Father Like Son

DOG DIARIES SERIES

Dog Diaries (*with Steven Butler*)
Happy Howlidays! (*with Steven Butler*)
Mission Impawsible (*with Steven Butler*)
Curse of the Mystery Mutt (*with Steven Butler*)
Camping Chaos! (*with Steven Butler*)
Dinosaur Disaster! (*with Steven Butler*)
Big Top Bonanza! (*with Steven Butler*)

THE I FUNNY SERIES

I Funny (*with Chris Grabenstein*)
I Even Funnier (*with Chris Grabenstein*)
I Totally Funniest (*with Chris Grabenstein*)
I Funny TV (*with Chris Grabenstein*)
School of Laughs (*with Chris Grabenstein*)
The Nerdiest, Wimpiest, Dorkiest I Funny Ever (*with Chris Grabenstein*)

MAX EINSTEIN SERIES

The Genius Experiment (*with Chris Grabenstein*)
Rebels with a Cause (*with Chris Grabenstein*)
Saves the Future (*with Chris Grabenstein*)
World Champions! (*with Chris Grabenstein*)

TREASURE HUNTERS SERIES

Treasure Hunters (*with Chris Grabenstein*)
Danger Down the Nile (*with Chris Grabenstein*)
Secret of the Forbidden City (*with Chris Grabenstein*)
Peril at the Top of the World (*with Chris Grabenstein*)
Quest for the City of Gold (*with Chris Grabenstein*)
All-American Adventure (*with Chris Grabenstein*)
The Plunder Down Under (*with Chris Grabenstein*)

HOUSE OF ROBOTS SERIES

House of Robots (*with Chris Grabenstein*)
Robots Go Wild! (*with Chris Grabenstein*)
Robot Revolution (*with Chris Grabenstein*)

JACKY HA-HA SERIES

Jacky Ha-Ha (*with Chris Grabenstein*)
My Life is a Joke (*with Chris Grabenstein*)

DANIEL X SERIES

The Dangerous Days of Daniel X (*with Michael Ledwidge*)
Watch the Skies (*with Ned Rust*)
Demons and Druids (*with Adam Sadler*)
Game Over (*with Ned Rust*)
Armageddon (*with Chris Grabenstein*)
Lights Out (*with Chris Grabenstein*)

OTHER ILLUSTRATED NOVELS

Kenny Wright: Superhero (*with Chris Tebbetts*)
Homeroom Diaries (*with Lisa Papademetriou*)
Word of Mouse (*with Chris Grabenstein*)
Pottymouth and Stoopid (*with Chris Grabenstein*)
Laugh Out Loud (*with Chris Grabenstein*)
Not So Normal Norbert (*with Joey Green*)
Unbelievably Boring Bart (*with Duane Swierczynski*)
Katt vs. Dogg (*with Chris Grabenstein*)
Scaredy Cat (*with Chris Grabenstein*)
Best Nerds Forever (*with Chris Grabenstein*)
Katt Loves Dogg (*with Chris Grabenstein*)

For more information about James Patterson's novels,
visit www.penguin.co.uk